Born in Edinburgh in 1906, **John Innes Mackintosh Stewart** was educated at Oriel College, Oxford, where he was presented with the Matthew Arnold Memorial Prize and named a Bishop Frazer's scholar. After graduation he went to Vienna to study Freudian psychoanalysis for a year.

His first book, an edition of Florio's translation of *Montaigne*, got him a lectureship at the University of Leeds. In later years he taught at the universities of Adelaide, Belfast and Oxford.

Under his pseudonym, Michael Innes, he wrote a highly successful series of mystery stories. His most famous character is John Appleby, who inspired a penchant for donnish detective fiction that lasts to this day. His other well-known character is Honeybath, the painter and rather reluctant detective, who first appeared in *The Mysterious Commission*, in 1975.

Stewart's last novel, *Appleby and the Ospreys*, appeared in 1986. He died aged eighty-eight.

D1637757

The Ampersand Papers
Appleby and Honeybath
Appleby and the Ospreys
Appleby At Allington
The Appleby File
Appleby On Ararat
Appleby Plays Chicken
Appleby Talking
Appleby Talks Again
Appleby's Answer
Appleby's End
Appleby's Other Story
An Awkward Lie
The Bloody Wood
Carson's Conspiracy
A Change of Heir
Christmas At Candleshoe
A Connoisseur's Case
The Daffodil Affair
Death At the Chase
Death At the President's Lodging
A Family Affair
From London Far
The Gay Phoenix

Going It Alone
Hamlet, Revenge!
Hare Sitting Up
Honeybath's Haven
The Journeying Boy
Lament For a Maker
Lord Mullion's Secret
The Man From the Sea
Money From Holme
The Mysterious Commission
The New Sonia Wayward
A Night of Errors
Old Hall, New Hall
The Open House
Operation Pax
A Private View
The Secret Vanguard
Sheiks and Adders
Silence Observed
Stop Press
There Came Both Mist and Snow
The Weight of the Evidence
What Happened at Hazelwood

MICHAEL INNES

THE LONG FAREWELL

HOUSE OF
STRATUS

This edition published in 2001 by House of Stratus, an imprint of
House of Stratus Ltd, Thirsk Industrial Park, York Road, Thirsk,
North Yorkshire, YO7 3BX, UK.

www.houseofstratus.com

Typeset by House of Stratus, printed and bound by Short Run Press Limited.

A catalogue record for this book is available from the British Library
and the Library of Congress.

ISBN 1-84232-742-9

1

PROLOGUE IN ITALY

'Tis here but yet confused:
Knavery's plain face is never seen till used.

Othello

1

'Come in!'

The summons was a cordial shout, and Appleby pushed open the door in the long, blank, wistaria-covered wall. It was a handsome pleasure-house, now in some decay, and all its windows were on the farther side, looking out westward over the lake. The sun was dropping towards Monte Caplone; Garda had turned from its midday blue to a white sheet of fire against which, for a moment, Appleby could see nothing except in silhouette. Even so, there was no mistaking Lewis Packford's astonishing bulk as it heaved itself up from a desk – nor the bellow of surprised laughter by which the movement was accompanied.

'Sir John, God save you!'

Sir John Appleby advanced and shook hands. He was well accustomed to Packford's greeting him with these Falstaffian allusions. They were entirely inapposite, for in middle age Appleby was still as spare as a sprinter, and it was Packford himself who could fairly be described as a tun of a man.

But Packford's humour was invariably pointless and boisterous. He knew Shakespeare by heart, and had a trick of quoting from him virtually at random. It would never enter your head that he was a man of intellectual capacity. He was vigorous and confident; he might well be clever; noticing that he appeared prosperous, you might suppose that he had somewhere built up a flourishing uncomplicated commercial concern. Actually he was a scholar, and there were people who maintained that he had one of the best brains in his field. Living privately – even rather secretively – and unhampered by such routine duties as fall to professors and their kind, he had achieved notable researches in the hinterland of Elizabethan literature, and time and again brought off some astonishing success. Commonly he contrived to give these a spectacular, even a sensational turn. There were some therefore who were inclined to shake their heads over Lewis Packford. He didn't really quite securely belong – this wayward elusive man who delighted childishly in showing off, in casting miserably into the shade the labours of colleagues less theatrically endowed, in springing some queer, disconcerting and impregnably documented surprise in the particular little learned world he had chosen as a stamping ground. He ought to be doing something else.

All this made Appleby find Packford interesting, and disposed him to renew from time to time a casual acquaintance begun some years before. Appleby was not a scholar but a policeman. He had in fact recovered for Packford some valuable documents which had been made off with by a rather specialized sort of burglar. And Packford had been grateful. He was almost certainly, Appleby supposed, a genuinely warm and generous man. If the two ran into each other in the street, Packford's large pale expanse of face would light up precisely as it had done now. And when Appleby had come to the top at Scotland Yard, Packford sent him a battered stave once carried – he declared – by that anonymous officer of the law whom the Lord Chief Justice had ordered to carry Sir John Falstaff to the Fleet.

'Well, well! And what in faith make you from Wittenberg?' Packford accompanied this question with a large clumsy gesture not at all suggestive of the cultivated Prince of Denmark.

'A truant disposition, no doubt.' Appleby smiled and threw his ancient Panama hat on a chair. 'I won't pretend that I left London with any idea of running you to earth.'

'Didn't you, now?' Packford seemed to find this disclaimer oddly amusing. 'You haven't brought a warrant, eh – or extradition papers, or whatever they are called?'

'Nothing of the sort, I'm afraid. And it's less a matter of running you to earth than of running you to water.' Appleby had walked over to a window. 'Good lord, what a view!'

'Splendid, isn't it?' Packford lumbered over to join him and stared out unseeingly. 'You can just spot Sirmione from the terrace. Sweet Catullus' all but island olive-silvery Sirmio. My God, Appleby –what a line!'

'Yes, indeed.' Appleby wasn't inclined to dispute this literary judgement. Probably Tennyson had never juggled his vowels and consonants to better effect in his life. But there wasn't the slightest reason to suppose that Packford possessed an atom of literary taste. That was part of the chap's fascination. All his investigations were totally ungoverned by the slightest awareness of the actual substance of the stuff he dealt with to such triumphant effect. The lady who enunciated the classic proposition that art is beautiful was own sister to Lewis Packford. In aesthetic matters the man's great bulk floated on a large full tide of vague enthusiasm. The stuff was by definition tiptop. Waving your arms, you received it with shouts of wonder and joy. And then you got down to a stiff bit of detective investigation next door to it. But even if the detective investigation hadn't been as good as anything the CID turns up, Appleby couldn't possibly have felt superior to Packford. The man rejoiced too much in the spirit of life that was in him.

'I was uncommonly lucky to pick up this place for the summer. You saw the villa?'

Appleby nodded. 'Your retainer in the kitchen told me you'd be down here. It's a nice place.'

'The villa's modest, of course – very modest. But this summer-house affair belongs to another age. It's rather grand, don't you think? I like *grotteschi* on my walls. All these little nudes like amorous shrimps. No vice in them, but lively. And this is the best position on the lake, if you ask me.'

'I think it well may be.' Appleby continued to admire the prospect. It was precisely like Packford, he thought, to take his large innocent pride in his casual acquisition for a season.

'Over there's no good at all.' Packford gestured vaguely towards the south-west. 'A sort of riviera, nowadays. But on this side you get hardly anybody. Even the road's the secondary one. German tourists coming over the Brenner tend to take it, of course, if they're making for Verona. You know Verona?'

'Yes – and I'm joining my wife there this evening.' Appleby turned away from the view to glance at Packford. It was second nature to him to catch any shade of significance in the tone of a voice. Had there been a faint enigmatical reverberation in Packford's as he named the city of the Montagues and Capulets? 'Do you go there much?' he asked.

'To Verona?' Packford looked extravagantly blank. 'Oh, no – not at all.'

'I'm told they filmed *Romeo and Juliet* largely in Siena. More undisturbed medieval settings than you get in Verona.'

'Ah, yes.' Packford again looked blank – but presently proceeded, almost conscientiously, to quotation. '*Two households, both alike in dignity,*' he declaimed, '*In fair Verona, where we lay our scene.* A wonderful idea, to open with a sonnet. And what a play!' Packford paused – and suddenly his features seemed to transform themselves and sharpen. 'But there's a great puzzle there, you know.'

'In *Romeo and Juliet*?'

'Bang in the sonnet Willy the Shake writes by way of prologue. Last line of the third quatrain.'

'I don't remember it.' To call Shakespeare Willy the Shake, Appleby was thinking, was the sort of prep. school facetiousness that it took a Packford to rejoice in.

'*Is now the two hours' traffic of our stage.*' Packford chuckled. 'Go to the Old Vic or to Stratford, my dear chap, and look at your watch when the curtain goes up. And remember that modern producers still make substantial cuts for performance. When the show's over, you'll realise that '*two hours' traffic*' takes some explaining.'

'Poetic licence, perhaps?'

'I don't think so. It's a real puzzle. I'll get at it one day.'

'But it's nothing of that sort you're at work on now?' Appleby made a gesture towards a large table piled high with books and papers.

'At work on?' Packford's glance followed Appleby's to the table, and then he shook his head. 'Oh, no – dear me, no. Just some dull stuff. But this is a good place for it. Quiet, as I was saying. Gets one away from – well, complications.' Packford paused on this, and then broke rather hurriedly into speech again. 'Just that old woman – who's a good cook by Italian standards – and her grandson to tidy up the garden. I forget the day of the week, and I never look at my watch.' As he said this, Packford took out his watch and studied it, so that Appleby reflected he was a man with that sort of blessed interior economy that is always joyfully expectant of its next meal. 'The little *vaporetto* punctuates the day. There it is, making for Torre del Benaco now. Garda was the Benacus of the Romans. You'll stop and have a bite? I never see an Englishman from month's end to month's end. Nor even an Englishwoman either. But then, as you know, I'm not a ladies' man.' At this, Packford suddenly roared with laughter.

Appleby smiled. The invitation hadn't been very felicitously phrased, but it was entirely cordial. 'I'll be very glad to,' he said. 'Judith's coming along the *autostrada* from Turin. Even if her car doesn't blow up, she won't get to Verona till quite late.'

'Then let's go up to the *villino*. The view's just as good from there, and we can get a drink. I keep none of the insidious stuff down here.' Packford wandered blunderingly about his summer-house, moving sundry objects meaninglessly from one place to another in a sort of ritual tidying-up for the day. 'What beats me,' he said, 'is how you tracked me down here, my dear fellow. There aren't more than three men in England who know of my having got hold of this little place. I'm in retirement, as they say.'

'As it happens, I know two of them – so there's no mystery in the matter.' Appleby added a word or two making good this claim. 'And this morning, when I was in Riva, I suddenly remembered what I'd been told. And I decided, of course, to get my dinner off you.'

'Then, come along. We'll see what old Giuseppina can do. Perhaps she can serve up her grandson in a collop – eh?' Packford laughed so unaffectedly at this fatuous witticism that it seemed really funny. 'Baked Gino pie. A trifling foolish banquet, as somebody somewhere says. But where? My memory's going, I'm afraid.'

'Wasn't it Verona?' And Appleby looked whimsically at his host. 'Your mind runs on the place, if you ask me.'

They walked up the long sloping garden through a faint breeze blowing gratefully off the lake. Gino, bare and browned to the waist, made a great business of removing a battered hat and standing respectfully attentive as they went past. Being unconscious of his employer's late horrific proposals in regard to him, he produced at the same time a dazzling smile. Packford was aware that the boy was entitled to notice; he stopped and in fluent ramshackle Italian gave him what were clearly the first random instructions to come into his head. But within seconds he was entirely absorbed in this occupation. Striding up and down, and pointing now in one direction and now another, he might have been the oldest-established of landed proprietors, effecting dispositions that would benefit his remote posterity.

It was impossible – Appleby again thought – not to warm to Packford. And young Gino obviously thought the world of him. There was a similar performance when they reached the house and Gino's grandmother appeared bobbing on the terrace. Packford's imbecile brand of humour must go very well into Italian, for when Giuseppina wasn't being tumultuously indignant over what was presumably the suggestion of sundry culinary impossibilities she was cackling with laughter. Then the conference turned serious. It was quite beyond Appleby's linguistic reach, but it went on for so long that one had to suppose a feast of enormous elaboration was being projected. Preparing it and eating it would both take so long that he wouldn't be in Verona till midnight. He rather regretted the perfectly idle impulse that had made him halt on the road to look up this eccentric man of learning.

Still, it was a lovely evening in a lovely place. They sat on the terrace and sipped, uncontaminated by gin, the sweet commonplace vermouth that draws such subtlety from its native air. But Packford wasn't built for the Italian climate, Appleby thought – and he didn't feel surprised when the massive figure opposite him produced a silk handkerchief and mopped his brow. 'My dear Appleby,' he murmured, 'how I envy you your well-preserved youth. And O, that this too too solid flesh would melt!'

'I doubt whether that would be very comfortable.'

Packford suddenly sat up. 'Do you know,' he demanded, 'that it's fashionable nowadays to accept the reading of the Good Quarto?'

Appleby smiled. 'No, I'm afraid I don't.'

'It's "sallied," you see. And they declare that to be a rare form of "sullied." Absolute nonsense, believe me.' Having got well on his hobbyhorse, Packford was animated. 'Hamlet, after all, is fat and scant of breath.'

'But haven't eminent persons – I do seem to remember this – declared that to be fat was merely to be sweaty?'

'Pitiful twaddle, my dear man. I think I can prove – I'm pretty certain I can prove – that Shakespeare's original Hamlet, who was of course Richard Burbage, weighed close to eighteen stone. Have you ever considered why *Hamlet* is so marvellous a play – such tremendous stuff?'

Appleby merely shook his head at this large question.

'Partly, at least, it's because Shakespeare had that wonderful inspiration of the delicate suffering soul in the great puffing wheezing body of a sedentary out-of-condition scholar.' Packford, as he announced his discovery, gently wheezed himself. 'Think of the effectiveness of it! Think of the effectiveness of the moment when the great man-mountain declares that Yorick used to carry him shoulder-high! Wonderful stuff, Appleby. And then the grave.'

'Ophelia's grave?'

'Exactly. Think of the episode of supreme savage comedy when Hamlet jumps into her grave and gets jammed in it.' Packford leant forward as he spoke, and his bulk blotted out the long line of tiny lights that had begun to prick the dusk from Salo to Gardone.

Appleby chuckled to himself in the dusk. *Oh, matter and impertinency mixed,* he said to himself. And Packford, he knew, loved linking a sober discovery to some extravagant hypothesis. When he was able to prove that Burbage was really a very fat man, all this would come out. Meanwhile, Packford relished keeping a discovery up his sleeve for a time. He had his regular technique for surprising the world. First the foolproof case, painfully elaborated and checked and polished in deep secrecy. Then the leak – so that one interested scholar heard uneasily from another that there was some reason to suppose Lewis Packford was at it again, was nursing this or that monstrously upsetting discovery. Then the swift unmasking of his design – in a long letter to *The Times Literary Supplement*, or in a small book attractively got up with telling illustrations, instantly commanding the attention of the fashionable metropolitan reviewers. Before the learned journals could lumber into reasoned appraisal, the whole thing had been accepted as gospel by the common reader and become established as a plain fact of literary history.

And almost certainly Packford was up to something of the sort now – although Appleby didn't really believe that it had much to do with the corpulence or otherwise of Richard Burbage. All this talk was a determined if light-hearted smokescreen put up by Packford to obscure some actual design. And Appleby thought he could take a dim guess at it.

This eminent literary detective wasn't in Italy for his health. Even if his own gross corpulence made it medically probable that he should drop down dead at any moment, such a calculation wouldn't make the slightest impact on Packford's sanguine personality. No – this wasn't a rest cure. Nor, for all his delight in his situation and his fluent chattering in Italian with his retainers, was it matter of a lover's retreat into communion with the soil and culture of his passion. Packford's wanderings, when they happened, were invariably strategic in conception. This villa was a cunningly chosen lurking place. And Packford, as he had virtually admitted, had been very far from advertising it. Mere chance had put Appleby in possession of his whereabouts. And perhaps – despite the cordiality of his welcome – he wasn't too pleased at being found out.

Not that Appleby felt in the least an intruder. If he now tumbled to some secret of Packford's, that would be all in the game, and Packford would acknowledge it as such. And indeed Appleby was determined – quite idly, indeed, since the whole matter was without seriousness of any sort – to discover what he could. Detective work of his own wasn't commonly his notion of a holiday. But detection that is all amid innocence and merely learned guile, that can't end in anybody being hanged or imprisoned or disgraced: well that, after all, was about as complete a change as he could run to. So he decided to have a go.

The little breeze had faded away, and when Giuseppina brought out candles they burned without a flicker in the warm, faintly lemon-scented air. It was an evening for dining *al fresco* – and, sure enough, the meal was presently brought out to them where they sat. It wasn't, after all, in the least elaborate: only a mess of deadly-looking but delicious *fungi*, followed by a chicken displaying a higher proportion of flesh to bone than is at all common south of the Alps. They drank Chianti. And Appleby tapped the flask. 'It's like the vermouth,' he said. 'Sit down with it in a dark room, and it would be undistinguished stuff. But here – well, it's another matter.'

'My dear man, Portia knew that. *Nothing is good, I see, without respect*. You remember?'

Appleby nodded. '*How many things by season season'd are* – isn't that it? – *to their right praise and true perfection!* I suppose it's true everywhere. But what about Shakespeare's having had it borne in upon him in Italy?'

Packford set down his glass with caution. 'Now just what,' he asked with great casualness, 'puts that in your head?'

'I'm sure I don't know. Would it be your Giuseppina's candles? Certainly they reminded me of Portia coming home to Belmont. *The light we see is burning in my hall; how far that little candle throws his beams*. And look over there.' Appleby pointed across the darkness of the lake. 'Those tiny lights on the farther shore. You could reach out your hand to them. I'd say there really is Italian air in that last act of *The Merchant of Venice*.'

'And therefore Shakespeare must actually have travelled across Europe and taken a sniff at it?' Packford leant back and laughed with great decision. 'Cobweb, my dear Appleby – mere cobweb! There's a great deal of English poetry that is stuffing with Greek air, if it comes to that. But how many great English poets have ever set eyes on Greece? Two, precisely.'

'So you think Shakespeare didn't come to Italy?'

'I didn't say that.'

'Ah.'

Packford looked suspiciously at his guest. 'I can see,' he said genially, 'that you've been reading some rubbish or other. There's enough of it, the Lord knows.'

Appleby shook his head. 'I don't read much in that sort of learned way. But didn't somebody lately find an old map of Verona, and decide that it fitted Shakespeare's Verona exactly?'

'There's no end to what people find it possible to decide – no end at all. He must have been to Venice, since he knew that business was transacted on the Rialto. It's all like that, the talk of Shakespeare in Italy. Crackpot stuff, like saying he must really have been Lord Tomnoddy, since otherwise he couldn't have made all those references to hunting and hawking and heraldry.' Packford reached comfortably for the Chianti flask. 'And, after all, does it much matter whether he travelled in Italy or not? The plays remain just as wonderful either way.'

'Oh, quite so.' Coming from Packford, it seemed to Appleby, this austere critical doctrine verged on the disingenuous. 'But I've known you pursue rather similar curiosities from time to time.'

Packford waved this aside. 'Mind you,' he said, 'there would be real critical interest in a related question. Did he know Italian? Could he read it? One would give something to be able to answer that.'

'I seem to remember being told that *Othello* is important there. Isn't it true that its only source was in Italian?'

'Ah, yes – Cintio's *Ecatommiti.*' Packford paused, as if his mind were wandering. 'But Cintio's yarn *may* have got translated into English, you know, without the translation's having survived. Or a translation into French may have come his way. There's an English ballad on the story. Unfortunately it's one of John Payne Collier's forgeries.' He chuckled. 'Now, there's a fascinating subject: the history of the great Shakespearian forgers! What a pity that it can't happen any more.'

Appleby was interested. 'But can't it? Why not?'

'Too many experts. Too much science.'

'Perhaps so. But expert knowledge, and the command of scientific techniques, can work both ways. In some fields I'm familiar with, the forger who commands them can put up quite an alarming show. It's rather as with warfare. Sometimes science puts the attack on top, and sometimes the defence. Of course I agree that nowadays there are certain directions in which the forger's liberty has been drastically curtailed. Think of Van Meegeren's spurious Vermeers and De Hooghs. There wasn't a chance for them once the chemists came along and spotted a resin of the phenolformaldehyde group, unknown until the last years of the nineteenth century. And it was the same with the most noted of the recent literary forgers, T J Wise.'

Packford shook his head. 'Not quite. Wise pretty well confined himself to the forging of nineteenth-century printed material. If he'd known enough on the scientific side, and taken enough trouble, he might have produced things that were indetectable. Or take inks. You or I could quite readily manufacture ink according to one or another of the methods current at, say, the beginning of the seventeenth century. And if we then used it cleverly and sparingly on paper preserved from that period – which isn't hard to come by in small quantity – the result would quite soon baffle the back-room boys in their labs. Conceivably in five years, certainly in twenty, the chemical situation would be tricky enough to produce divided opinions.'

11

'Always provided that materials from organic sources weren't much involved. It's no longer possible to tell fibs by the century, so to speak, where the new carbon tests can be brought in. Think how they've vindicated the antiquity of the Dead Sea Scrolls.' Appleby paused. There was a new delicious smell on the terrace. It was evident that Giuseppina knew how to make coffee. 'But hasn't it always been possible,' he asked, 'to tell simply by the smell? If, I mean, you really knew your stuff. Amateurs of literature all over Europe fell for Macpherson's Ossian, but it didn't take in a professional like Dr Johnson. Chatterton was a marvellous boy, and his Rowley poems impressed the respectable antiquaries of Bristol. But he was sunk as soon as they were put into the hands of a poet and scholar like Gray. Ireland could turn out anything of Shakespeare's, from a signature to a whole play. All sorts of persons of rank and consequence believed in them, but a high-powered authority like Edmund Malone at once knew them to be ridiculous.'

Packford was producing a box of cigars. 'There's something in all that,' he said. 'But it's not always so. Van Meegeren's things took in tremendous pundits.'

'But largely, I think, because it was war-time. A competent *expertise* in a field like that is a matter of very delicate intellectual and aesthetic judgements. If you had to be smuggled past a lot of Nazi guards in order to look at a painting, your responses to it might be affected in queer ways... No brandy, thank you. I've quite a bit of driving in front of me still.'

'No doubt you're wise – although it's a good road.' Rather reluctantly, Packford pushed away the bottle he had been offering. 'We've hit, you know, on a complex subject. The moral issues are sometimes far from clear. Take Chatterton. His fakes were scarcely fakes to him. He lived in a medieval dream-world of his own contriving, and the poems and so forth came out of it. Make-believe was a condition of the functioning of his genius – and it was a very real genious. It's arguable that it was the duty of society to sustain him in his delusions.'

'As it is, his story's unbearable.' Appleby was silent for a moment. Packford, he was reflecting, had turned quite serious. At the same time, he was discernibly distrait – as if, despite the genuineness of his hospitable impulse, some insistent preoccupation was tugging at his mind. Appleby resolved to get away fairly soon. 'Yes,' he presently went on, 'it's a complex subject, as you say. And it certainly sometimes puzzles the law. One doesn't commit a crime in teaching oneself to paint precisely like Richard Wilson in the morning, and precisely like Renoir in the afternoon. But it would be an unlikely routine to adopt in the disinterested pursuit of an artistic education. I'd turn a bit suspicious, prowling round a studio which showed a set-up like that.'

Packford laughed. 'Suspicion's your job, Appleby. And it's a good part of my job too. They say I'm credulous, you know. But it's not true. I'll admit to having run a notion or two of my own pretty hard, and to squeezing my evidence as if I were a barrister out for a verdict. From time to time I may even have put across a pretty tall story. But I'm not aware that I've ever been taken in. I've never, as they say, been had.' And again Packford laughed – confidently, infectiously. 'Good luck to the chap who tries!'

Giuseppina had come to clear away the meal. The two men rose and strolled up and down the terrace. 'But it's not the technique of forgery that's really fascinating,' Packford said. 'It's the psychology.'

'I'd say there are a dozen psychologies.'

'Exactly! And there's what you might call a *gradus*, too. I mean that there are degrees of the impulse. At one end there's no more than what might be called a bit of historical sense and curiosity – the prompting, say, to try out the way some earlier painter has applied his glazes or managed his edges. Further along, you come on chaps with whom the thing has gone obsessive and passionate. Think of the Venus of Milo, Appleby! A masterpiece of the fifth century before Christ – a masterpiece, that's to say, of the great age of that sort of thing. Only it happens to be nothing of the kind. It was created some four hundred years later. Why? It was a vision of the goddess that can't have cut any ice with that later age. Her vital statistic would have appeared all wrong.'

'Not, perhaps, to a patron of antiquarian mind. The statue may have been commissioned by some first-century gentleman who thought modern art terribly vulgar.'

'No, no – nothing of the kind.' Packford could be brusquely dismissive without being in the least offensive. 'The Venus of Milo mayn't be all that our grandparents cracked her up to be. But she's far too good to be a piece of historical pastiche done to order with an eye on a rich man's cheque-book. It's a case of an artist's passionate identification with the vision of another age.'

'Or perhaps it's a joke.' Appleby couldn't resist the impulse to receive Packford's large vague enthusiasms sceptically. 'For there, I think, you often find the master motive behind fakes and forgeries. It can be the underlying motive, even when the superficial motive is predatory, practical and financial. I mean the impulse to extract fun out of laughing up one's sleeve.'

'Laughing up one's sleeve?' Packford repeated the words as if they were entirely obscure to him. And then, disconcertingly, he gave one of his shouts of laughter. 'Yes, of course – it would be enormous fun! But, do you know, I never thought of it?'

'There seems to be a particular attraction in the idea of fooling people who are inclined to patronize you. Something of the sort certainly operated in Wise's case. He was a prosperous man, and he had collected a library of great value and interest, which scholars were eager to consult. He was therefore surrounded by learned people paying court to him – and at the same time unconsciously treating him rather *de haut en bas*, since he was only an eccentric commercial person, after all, unprovided with the unspeakable blessings of a classical education. Well, he fooled them to the top of their bent. And how he must have enjoyed it!'

Once more Packford laughed – this time so loudly that even Giuseppina, who must have been well accustomed to these explosions, turned round and stared. 'Yes, of course,' he said. 'I can see

that. And he must have felt like Chaucer's Manciple. You remember?'
And striding down his terrace, Packford began to chant:

> 'Now is nat that of God a ful fair grace,
> That switch a lewed mannes wit shal pace
> The wisdom of an heep of lerned men?'

Giuseppina gestured expressively to the heavens. She had a high
regard for her employer, but this clearly didn't preclude her regarding
him as a little touched. *Pazzo* would be the word. And perhaps –
Appleby thought – there really was an element of some strangeness
in Packford. If, one day, something very surprising turned up about
him, you wouldn't – so to speak – be very surprised. And yet this
circumstance – that you wouldn't be surprised by a surprise – was
surprising in itself. It couldn't quite be accounted for, that was to say,
in the light of what seemed the normal large transparency of
Packford: the simplicity of his vanities and enthusiasms which
blended so naturally, somehow, with the keenness and vigour of his
mind.

Did he, perhaps, have a secret life? Briefly, as they paused at the far
end of the terrace to gaze again at the faint lights across the lake,
Appleby tried to equip him with something of the sort. But the
exercise came to nothing. There was no glimpse, for instance, of
anything out of the way in this small temporary household
established in so pleasant a place.

Perhaps Packford's only oddity consisted in his being something
of a survivor from a past age. There weren't many of his sort about.
There were of course dilettantes, wealthy or merely prosperous, in
plenty. English, American, Australian, you found them scattered over
Italy and the south of France. But nowadays that sort of person's
fancy seemed to lie nearly always in the fine arts or in music.
Corresponding amateurs of literature – at least of an ability and
pertinacity sufficient to gain them serious scholarly consideration –
were much harder to find. It wasn't a field that Appleby knew
particularly well, or had much occasion for interest in. But at least he

couldn't think of a single other person in precisely Packford's situation. He had money, but he travelled light. He was presumably unmarried, and Appleby had never heard him mention even a distant relation. He could entirely please himself. And what was pleasing him now – if Appleby hadn't guessed entirely wrong – was the persuasion that he was going to prove William Shakespeare of Stratford-upon-Avon to have been at one time a traveller in Italy. Milan, Mantua, Verona, Padua, Venice: they all had their Shakespearian associations – and to one of Packford's temperament and reputation the possibility of unearthing and displaying to the world an actual biographical link would be irresistibly appealing. To present himself before the learned with what he had called mere cobweb triumphantly transmuted to perdurable steel; to flourish before their noses, it might be, the dramatist's very hotel-bill on the Grand Canal: that would be precisely Packford's cup of tea.

And the ambition was at least blessedly innocent. It wasn't even frivolous – or not if you took the scholar's view of the dignity inherent in adding to any and every sort of knowledge. It didn't make you a nuisance or a blight to others, and it didn't land you in any trouble. And there was much – Appleby thought – to be said for any activity which was quite unlikely to add to the burdens of the police.

As he made this prosaic professional reflection Appleby became aware that his host was again looking at his watch. This time, it could scarcely be in expectation of a meal; and the plain inference was either that he had an appointment or that he wanted to get back to work. Whatever the nature of that pile of books and documents down in his summer-house, he would be quite glad to get back to them. 'I must be getting on my way,' Appleby said. 'I go round by Peschiera, I suppose, and that makes it quite a step.'

'You must really be moving on?' Packford asked. He now seemed genuinely reluctant to lose his guest. 'Well, it was uncommonly kind of you to look me up in this solitude. And we've had a good talk.' He laughed. 'And talk taking an odd turn, as good talk should. What about our going into partnership, Appleby, eh? Shall we set up together?'

'Detecting forgeries?'

'No, no. That would be too easy, my dear chap – too easy altogether. Let's set up, you and I, at presenting the world with some handsome ones. We'd be a tiptop combination, you know. How shall we begin?'

Packford's freakish humour was coming on top again. He had asked his question with a great appearance of gravity. 'It must depend,' Appleby said, 'on the state of the market. I shan't be one of those disinterested forgers, taking out all his dividend in a quiet laugh. Indeed, I think I'll concentrate on sales.' He paused, rather flogging his brain for a way in which to keep up for a further civil minute or two this laboured facetiousness from which his host seemed to obtain such harmless pleasure. 'But is there really much of a market to tap – I mean, for purely literary forgery? Is there anything like the big money that the high-powered artistic variety can command? I'd hardly have thought so.'

'Tons of it, my dear chap.' Packford in this mood, Appleby reflected, probably spoke largely at random. 'America, you know. Public institutions with vast resources would positively compete for anything right at the top. Private collectors, too. Of course, there aren't so many of them as go in for pictures and furniture and porcelain and so forth. Still, they're there. Some quite sane, and some a bit round the bend. But then, my sort's a bit mad, too, wouldn't you say? Why do I mole away after obscure events of no large human interest – of no genuine intellectual interest at all – back in the seventeenth century?'

Packford had paused, almost as if puzzled at hearing himself turn serious again. 'You know,' he went on, 'the plain man's answer: that I've found a tolerably harmless way of keeping myself out of the pub. Of the pub and – well – other things in that general area. But the devil of it is, you know, that it may let a chap down. A chap may feel he's been missing things.' Packford shook his head; he seemed suddenly depressed. 'And get into a scrape, eh? Rebound, as they say.'

'No doubt.' Appleby was puzzled before this somewhat incoherent vein.

'And, of course, it's simply chance that takes one in the first place into one manner of life rather than another. And one looks back, and imagines one might have chosen better – whereas, really and truly, choice didn't enter into the matter. What do you think?'

Appleby thought only that the hour was too advanced to enter upon a discussion of the mildly perplexing problem of necessity and free will. 'What sort of career,' he asked rather at random, 'would you now fancy entering upon, supposing you were thirty years younger?'

'Busting atoms, probably. Or perhaps being a professional amorist. You remember the name of Edward Dowden? Not a bad Shakespeare critic, in an old-fashioned way. Well, after a long life of blameless scholarship, he confessed that what he would really have liked to be was the lover of many women. A bit frightening, wouldn't you say?'

'Possibly so. And if he'd put in that long lifetime simply pursuing wenches, he'd no doubt have looked back and said his only true ambition had been to be a great scholar.'

'I suppose there's a happy mean.' Packford laughed again – but this time it was a short nervous laugh that seemed unlike him. 'But these desires are all diseases, damn them. Scholarship – that's a disease. Browning's Grammarian died of it. And sex – that's a disease too. Either can make an idiot of you, so that you positively stare at yourself.'

They were standing beside Appleby's car, so that there was now a distinct awkwardness in parting upon this obscurely confessional note. For it was certainly that. Packford, who seemed to have been living for some time in a very solitary way, had been prompted to reveal some present preoccupation in a manner that he would no doubt later regret. 'I must step on it,' Appleby said, 'or Judith will be in Verona hours before me.'

'And that wouldn't do? I see you're the experienced married man. I've sometimes thought of having a shot at it. But here I am – finding Giuseppina and Gino quite enough to cope with.'

'I suppose you may spring a surprise on us one day. It's your habit, after all.' Appleby shook hands, and climbed into the car. It was a rather queerly abrupt leave-taking – the more so because of the darkness into which his host immediately vanished. Appleby had a single brief impression of him, lumbering rapidly back to his summer-house, as if he had a tryst in it.

He was never to see Lewis Packford alive again.

2

DEVELOPMENT AT URCHINS

Farewell, farewell… Why did I marry?

Othello

1

It was over Lewis Packford's open grave that Appleby first became aware of Mr Rood. One could tell at once – perhaps simply by the way he held his silk hat – that Mr Rood was an old hand at funerals. Indeed, if he hadn't so obviously belonged to the higher professional classes it would have been reasonable to suppose that he was in charge of the lay and technical part of the proceedings.

It was only later, of course, that Appleby learnt his name; and the thing mightn't have happened as it did but for the fact that it came on to rain hard. The heavy drops could be heard plonking on the coffin with a small hollow sound – as if the undertakers had inadvertently provided something a size too large even for Packford's enormous bulk. There was scarcely, it seemed to Appleby, a soul present who had any substantial occasion for private grief. And this, together with the weather, imported a certain element of mere dismalness to the burial. The dead man wouldn't have liked it. Appleby could almost hear him shouting clumsy jokes about maimed rites and churlish priests.

The service ended and the mourners dispersed. Appleby, who knew none of them, walked off alone under his umbrella. Outside the cemetery, he waited at a bus-stop. So – also under an umbrella – did the man presently to be revealed as Mr Rood. But Mr Rood didn't appear to think that their late joint concern put Appleby and himself on speaking terms; and as he had some appearance of being the older man Appleby held his tongue. The rain increased; there wasn't a bus; the rest of the funeral party seemed to have made a superior order of departure in private conveyances. Once Mr Rood dipped his umbrella to take a glance at the heavens, and the rain went plonk on his silk hat just as it had done on Packford's coffin. Mr Rood made an impatient clicking noise with his tongue – perhaps because of this, or perhaps at the insufficiencies of London's transport. Then a cruising taxi appeared, and Mr Rood with great promptitude agitated his umbrella. The taxi drew to the kerb. And at last Mr Rood spoke. 'Would you care, sir,' he asked politely, 'to share my cab?'

Appleby agreed, and the two men compared destinations and climbed in. They had travelled some hundreds of yards before Mr Rood spoke. 'A melancholy occasion,' he said. His tone contrived to emphasize the bleakly conventional character of this utterance.

'Yes indeed.'

There was a long silence. 'Distressing circumstances.' Mr Rood uttered this with a high degree of rock-like impassivity.

'Yes.'

Mr Rood applied himself to gently shaking out his umbrella on the floor of the cab – but with a very proper punctiliousness in regard to Appleby's legs. 'My name is Rood,' he said. 'I was the dead man's solicitor.'

'My name is Appleby.'

'How do you do.' The inflection which Mr Rood gave this was far from interrogative, and he sank back gloomily in his corner of the cab. Appleby conjectured – without any marked sense of deprivation – that he had now achieved as close an intimacy with the late Lewis Packford's solicitor as was to be permitted him. But in this he was wrong. 'Balance of the mind disturbed,' Rood presently said. 'A theological rather than a legal fiction. Senseless – but little harm in it, save in cases where the deceased person had made some quite recent change in testamentary dispositions.'

'Which I suppose Packford hadn't done.'

Since this hadn't been in the least a fishing remark, Appleby wasn't convinced that it deserved to be met with the massive effect of silence which Rood now achieved. However, having thus sufficiently vindicated his professional discretion, the solicitor did proceed in a more conversable vein. 'Not that I regard with any disfavour the spectacle of people of property making changes in their wills from time to time. From the solicitor's point of view, it is grist to the mill, after all. And there is much to be said for having the courage to change one's mind. Napoleon, you will recall, was celebrated for his ability decisively to alter his plans at short notice.'

'So I've heard.' Appleby wondered whether the correct and dim Mr Rood cherished a fantasy life in which he directed vast armies across the surface of Europe. 'And I imagine, by the way, that Lewis Packford was the sort of man who would, on occasion, do odd and impulsive things. And suicide is no doubt commonly a matter of sudden impulse.'

'It may be so. But I was a good deal surprised.'

'By Packford's taking that course?'

'Precisely. And I am a good deal surprised still.' Mr Rood contrived to lend to this statement the suggestion that it was itself surprising. The implication seemed to be that he wasn't often surprised, since his sagacity commonly penetrated with perfect accuracy into the future. 'I am assured by Packford's physician that our friend had no rational occasion to fear for his health. And, knowing him as I did, I cannot believe that he had any irrational prompting that way, either. No morbid fears about his interior economy, or anything of that sort.'

Appleby nodded. 'I should be inclined to agree with you. As it happens, I paid him a visit in Italy not long ago. He appeared to be in excellent health, and enjoying life. But it's my experience that, unless one is really intimate with a man, one may be entirely deceived about – well, his emotional constitution and underlying nervous condition. But perhaps you *were* an intimate?'

Rood, who during this speech had changed his position in the cab and was now eyeing Appleby attentively, shook his head slightly. 'Dear me, no. Nothing of the sort. Our association, it is true, extended beyond my professional services to him. I have, as it happens, a modest interest in certain of the subjects upon which he was so distinguished an authority. We even collaborated two or three times in papers on bibliographical and palaeographical topics. But I cannot claim much acquaintance with poor Packford's personal life. I speak from a very general impression. Still, it surprises me, I repeat, that he should take a revolver and blow his brains out.'

'You mean, Mr Rood, that the circumstance appears to you to deserve a good deal of investigation?'

Rather unexpectedly – but in a fashion that was entirely grim – Rood smiled. 'It will be proper for me to say,' he said with august formality, 'that I should not now be opening the subject at all, had not your being good enough to mention your name put me, Sir John, in full possession of your identity.'

'Ah.' Appleby was slightly disconcerted. 'But I have no official slant on this, you know. Although Packford has for some reason been buried in London, I understand he died in the country. It's very unlikely to be brought to me.'

'Quite so, quite so.' Rood spoke as one man who has adequate subordinates does to another. 'I had no thought of anything of the sort. And you will not think, Sir John, that one with a good deal of experience, however humdrum, as a family solicitor is at all likely to judge a respectable client's sudden suicide as a propitious occasion for detective investigation. Far from it. Ten to one, it is highly desirable that any such incident, however mysterious, should pass unexplored into oblivion.'

'I'm afraid that, professionally, it would be a little hard for me to agree to that.' Appleby smiled. 'But I see what you mean.'

'If the dead man were being blackmailed – well, he can be blackmailed no longer, and the last thing that his shade could desire would be a scandal. And to other common probabilities, similar considerations apply. But with poor Packford, I am in some little difficulty.'

'Difficulty?' Appleby asked.

'I cannot feel very confident that he did take his own life.' Rood delivered himself of this opinion entirely without emphasis or excitement. 'In fact, I should suppose it highly probable that he was murdered.'

Appleby was to reflect afterwards that he had been too hastily and baselessly sceptical about the surprising notion which had thus erupted in the mind of Mr Rood. The solicitor had undoubtedly a vein of conceit which might lead him to evolve and push pet theories. But he didn't appear hare-brained. And Appleby at this stage knew very little about the actual circumstances of Packford's death and presumed suicide; he had no facts with which instantly to controvert his casually acquired companion of the taxi-cab. But he knew from long experience that almost every suicide, however transparent, starts talk of foul play somewhere; and that it is not always in the temperamentally obvious individuals that such fantasies of homicide are found to have originated. The present probability, he instantly judged, was simply that Packford's unexpected death had touched off some quirk in Rood's mind, and set him imagining things.

But all this didn't mean that the suggestion could be politely ignored. Rood couldn't have been Packford's solicitor if he were not a responsible lawyer of good standing; nursing this suspicion, he had tumbled quite by accident into the company of Appleby, who was an Assistant Commissioner of the Metropolitan Police. It didn't follow that it was at all incumbent upon Appleby to get out a magnifying glass and begin hunting for bloodstains and footprints. Indeed, he wasn't entitled to. But he must attend to whatever information he was about to receive, and take appropriate action should it be necessary. 'I am greatly concerned,' he said, 'that you should have arrived at such a suspicion. But you have no doubt communicated it to the police-force concerned?'

'I certainly communicated one opinion I had formed to the officer who investigated the matter. Unfortunately, it has been virtually ignored. The police – and, I understand, the coroner – are entirely easy in their minds. The inquest has been adjourned. But I have no doubt that it will conclude in mere formality. Well, perhaps it is better so.' Mr Rood delivered himself of this final judgement with gloomy dignity.

'It is certainly nothing of the kind, if there is the slightest ground for any doubt in the matter.' Appleby spoke with some severity. 'Are you in a position to point to any motive which may have prompted to Packford's murder?'

'Robbery, Sir John.'

Appleby shook his head. 'I'm at some disadvantage, you know, because I am simply without the facts of the case. But in this country there are singularly few murders which are conceived of as deliberately incident to a robbery. Thieves and burglars commonly kill only when surprised, and then the circumstances are likely to leave no doubt about the matter.'

'It may well be that I am entirely mistaken.' Judging his umbrella now tolerably dry, Rood had begun to roll it with meticulous care. 'But the robbery of Packford, if it took place, was of a singular kind. I think you said you visited him in Italy?'

The taxi-cab bumped to a stop. It was in a traffic jam. Appleby glanced curiously at his companion. Rood had finished fiddling with his umbrella and was sitting with it upright between his knees. If he was a crank, his appearance was far from suggesting the fact. Looked at in a sufficiently wide context, he would no doubt appear dim. Viewed simply in the light of his profession, he suggested a dry narrow rigour which would make him entirely adequate at his job. 'Yes,' Appleby said, 'I did call on Packford in Italy during the summer. It was no more than a surprise visit. I had dinner with him, and then drove on to Verona.'

'I think that would have been on the 8th of July?'

The jerk with which Appleby sat up wasn't altogether a matter of the sudden renewed forward movement of the taxi. 'That was certainly the date,' he said. 'But I'd hardly have thought that it was an occasion to go down in history.'

'Ah.' There was a new tone in Rood's voice. It could easily be identified as satisfaction. 'There would be nothing remarkable in my knowing, without your having told me, about your call on Packford at Garda. But it's queer that I should know the date – eh?' He gave a conceited chuckle.

'There's nothing actually strange about it, I suppose. But it is mildy surprising. It's something that Packford might have mentioned to you, or to anyone, on his return to England. But one would hardly expect him to mention the precise date of so unimportant an event, or that it should then stick in your head. I had to make an effort myself to check that you'd got it right.'

'Quite so.' Rood was now really gratified. 'As a matter of fact, I learnt about it at the time. Packford and I were in correspondence during the summer – legal correspondence, you will understand, but with the usual more personal postscripts and so on which it is customary and courteous to add in such circumstances. He mentioned your call. He said that it came within an ace of being a celebration.' Rood paused. 'Does that strike you as entirely enigmatical?'

'I'm not sure that's a question to answer out of hand.' Appleby made this reply almost automatically. Where his official activities were in question it was a second nature to him to ask far more questions than he answered.

'I thought it possible that he might have mentioned to you the name of a certain member of a noble family in Verona.'

'We certainly had some talk about a lady living somewhere near Venice – and also, I think, about a foreigner of some distinction naturalized there. I don't know about Verona. My memory's rather vague. But I think it possible, as a matter of fact, that there was some mention of a couple of families in that city. And noble families, no doubt – although with domestic habits rather on the bourgeois side.'

For a moment Rood looked offended. This nonsense plainly disconcerted him and that was something he didn't like. Then he produced a short mirthless laugh. 'Montagues and Capulets,' he said. 'Very good...ha-ha! Poor Packford would certainly not keep away from Shakespeare for long. But my reference was to – um – a living gentleman of Verona. An impoverished aristocrat, Sir John, from whom Packford was in the expectation of buying something. But this, mark you, is only inference on my part. Packford was accustomed to being very close in matters of that sort. Or perhaps I ought to say that he was accustomed simultaneously to being very close and to dropping small tantalizing clues to his activities. Possibly "clues" is too technical a word, and trespasses on your own preserves. But, since you knew Packford, you will understand me.'

Appleby certainly did understand. It had been Packford's habit to stimulate curiosity by carefully dropped hints of coming discoveries – hints which were vague at first and then gained in definition as the moment for actually springing his next surprise on the learned world grew imminent. 'Did you discover,' he asked, 'just what it was that Packford hoped to get hold of on this occasion?'

'Far from it. I might have known nothing at all about it, had not Packford been in need of money.' Rood hesitated, as if conscious of the extreme gravity of thus beginning to divulge certain of his late client's private affairs. 'Not in the least a large sum of money, having regard to Packford's ample means. The difficulty was simply over obtaining foreign exchange for a purpose which he wasn't at all willing to declare. His banker had felt obliged to raise some objection to putting the matter through. He called upon me to arrange it, which I did. In a perfectly legal manner, I need hardly say.'

'I wonder what you mean by "not in the least a large sum of money"? To a modest traveller like myself, such an expression would cover anything up to about fifty pounds.'

'Quite so, Sir John. And it would be so with myself, precisely. In this instance, it was a thousand pounds. Packford required that, apart from the normal expenses of his summer's sojourn in Italy.'

'With which to buy something from an impoverished nobleman of Verona? I suppose there are such people?'

Rood laughed – this time with something like genuine enjoyment. 'It is exactly the question I asked myself, my dear Sir John. He sounded uncommonly shadowy, not to say fictitious. And Packford was – um – nothing if not vague about the whole thing. In another man, his attitude might fairly have been called shifty. But in Packford one could not disapprove of it. His temperament is no doubt known to you. He took great joy in his manner of going to work so as to astonish the learned. He had an instinct, you might say, for concealment.'

Appleby nodded. 'I think that's true. I've even wondered whether he carried it into other aspects of his life.'

'Um.' Rood made his ejaculation sound extremely discreet. 'At least I think we may say this. It was childish, perhaps. But endearing.' He accompanied these words with a return to his rockiest manner, as if to make it quite apparent that endearment existed for him only as an abstraction. 'The question is, did it all lead to his death.'

'Well, that appears to be *your* question. But I can't say, Mr Rood, that you've made out so much of a case, so far. If, that is to say, making out a case is what you're about.'

Rood looked offended again; he was certainly touchy. 'No doubt it sounds nebulous,' he said stiffly. 'But at least I believe that Packford acquired something of great interest and importance from this person in Verona' – he gave his mirthless laugh – 'whether noble or otherwise.'

'And you think this occurred quite recently?'

'I conclude, Sir John, that it occurred probably on the very night of your happening to visit him in July. He didn't mention anybody of the sort, whether by name or otherwise?'

'I'm certain he didn't.' Appleby was becoming rather impatient of Rood's mystery-mongering. 'Apart from his housekeeper and gardener – and, yes, my own wife – we didn't talk about any living persons at all.'

'But would you say that Packford was in any state of expectation?'

Appleby took a moment to consider this. 'Well, yes,' he said. 'I did get some rather indefinite impression of that sort.'

'Exactly!' Rood was once more cheerful. 'If you ask me, Packford was then in the hourly expectation of doing a highly secret and confidential deal with this fellow from Verona. And he must actually have succeeded in doing so by the following day. The manner of his referring to you as having just missed a celebration admits, to my mind, of no other explanation.'

Appleby was silent for a moment. It had certainly been true that the thought of Verona had held some special significance for Packford on that not-far-distant July evening. So far, in fact, Rood's

31

speculations were not unpersuasive. But they seemed to have only the haziest connection with the suspicion which he had propounded. 'And it's your idea,' Appleby asked, 'that Packford, having made this important acquisition in Italy, brought it back to this country, and was then robbed of it by someone who killed him in the process?'

But at this moment the cab stopped. 'Ah,' Rood said. 'My destination.' He peered at the taximeter. 'I shall give the man four shillings. If, that is to say, you judge such an arrangement to be equitable.' And he made to open the door beside him.

Appleby was surprised. Rood, who had seemed so determined to press upon him an unsolicited and bizarre speculation, was frankly bolting. Perhaps he had remembered that Napoleon made some rapid retreats. Or perhaps, on second thoughts, his resolution had failed him. And now he was already out on the pavement. But he hesitated. 'I ought to have arranged my thoughts,' he said. 'It is, after all, very unfamiliar ground. Perhaps, should I consider it justifiable to do so, I may communicate with you?'

'Certainly.' Appleby was definite but unenthusiastic. 'Write or ring up. There will be no difficulty in getting through to me.'

Rood nodded, and closed the door. But he was still hesitating, and a moment later he opened it again. 'Four-and-six,' he said. 'I decided to give four-and-six. I had omitted to consider the tip. Good afternoon.'

Rood banged the taxi door to again, turned, and hurried away. He had neglected to put up his umbrella. And Appleby's inward ear heard the rain once more plonking on his silk hat, as it had plonked on the coffin of Lewis Packford.

2

Whether or not Mr Rood thought fit to come forward with more information or surmise, the matter couldn't, it seemed to Appleby, be precisely dropped. Were he to take no action, and then some independent turn of affairs demonstrate that the solicitor hadn't been talking nonsense, he would himself scarcely appear in the light of one who had set a very striking example of vigilance to his subordinates of the Metropolitan Police.

But, even apart from this, he felt prompted to do something. He hadn't been a close friend of the dead man's. But he had liked him, and had happened to seek him out not so very long before he died. To Appleby's mind this meant that there would be a mild impiety in now continuing to take the manner of that death for granted. If a man is murdered, his shade is presumably grateful for being vindicted from the charge of suicide.

At the same time, Appleby felt another and simpler impulse – an impulse but for the constant strength of which within him he would probably be indifferently adorning quite another walk of life. He was curious about the business: curious about Packford; curious about Rood; and curious, above all, about that tenuous personal involvement in the supposed mystery constituted by his evening on Lake Garda not long ago. He spent the rest of his taxi journey trying to feel himself back more securely, more sensitively, into that. The result wasn't very satisfactory.

There undoubtedly had been some sort of expectation or distraction present at that simple feast, and there had also been some personal preoccupation in a sphere where one wouldn't have expected it. But Appleby found that his memory possessed no instrument with which to measure these things with any accuracy. Sharp but irrelevant sensuous impressions were what chiefly remained from that occasion: the brown torso of the boy Gino and his flashing smile; the fungi and the acid Tuscan wine; the lake turning to a long sheet of light as the sun sank. He had, after all, been very much on holiday. Perhaps he hadn't at all noticed the right things.

When he got back to Scotland Yard his first inquiry produced a surprise. The death of Lewis Packford, although taking place in Dorset, had been investigated by Detective-Inspector Cavill. It wasn't at once clear why it had been promoted to that busy officer's regard, and Appleby sent down a message that he'd be glad to find out.

Charles Cavill was in the building and appeared at once. He didn't look too pleased; he contrived to infuse a good deal of gloom into the simple business of handing Appleby a file; and he was unnecessarily formal and civil.

'I'm sorry to take up your time,' Appleby said. There were always these difficulties in a place that was neither quite one thing nor yet quite another, in which the set-up might be called quasi-military. Appleby had had his stiff periods; had weathered, as he made his way up the ladder, phases of resentment quite as acute as if he had come in at a high level from elsewhere. There had been times when it would have been extremely rash to indulge in apologetic murmurs. But he took all that very easily now; he was almost through, after all; he'd say what came into his head – and let them react, bless them, any way they chose. 'Yes,' he repeated. 'Terribly sorry, Cavill. But the fact is I knew this fellow Packford. It isn't long since I visited him in Italy and had dinner with him.'

'Indeed, sir.' Cavill's tone indicated that he didn't himself belong to a class of society that went gallivanting about the continent.

'And he seemed quite all right then. A great barrel of a man, but full of life, and with all sorts of forward-looking plans in his head. He was going to surprise people. Not a lot of people. Just a good many learned people. That was his line.'

'Yes, sir. I did gather that he appeared pretty harmless.' Cavill's voice now had a hint of weariness which Appleby instantly told himself was not necessarily meant to be offensive. Nobody in the whole place worked harder than Charles Cavill. And if he had concluded that there was no reason to suppose anything particularly sinister about Packford's death he now had a right to feel a little irritated, anyway.

'So I was surprised,' Appleby went on, 'to learn that the poor chap had blown his brains out. It's uncommon, you'll agree, when a man's looking actively ahead to this and that.'

'That's certainly true.' Cavill now spoke with decent professional briskness. 'But even a man who is absorbingly interested in life may make away with himself, provided that something bad enough turns up on him suddenly. The suddenness is important, I've often found. But perhaps I'm wrong. Of course you've had much more experience than I have, sir.'

Appleby sighed slightly. This unnecessary excursus hadn't even the justification of truth. Cavill's experience would fill whole filing-cabinets. Indeed, that was just what it did in a large unbeautiful fireproof room downstairs. 'Well then,' Appleby said with sudden sharp challenge, 'what about Packford? Is there any sign of something pretty bad bobbing up on him? He blew his brains out. What was it in aid of, anyway?'

'Page four,' Cavill said.

Page four was the last in the file. Cavill hadn't thought it necessary to compile extensive notes on Packford. Appleby glanced at the first sentence. 'Married!' he exclaimed. 'He kept uncommonly dark about it, I must say.'

'He had reason to,' Cavill said grimly. 'Read on.'

'Married again!' Appleby scanned the page for a moment and then put down the file. 'Well, I'm damned,' he said.

'Quite so, sir. It must be surprising – about somebody you knew quite well.'

'I didn't say that, Cavill. I've never, for instance, been near the place I know Packford had in the country. I've dined with him from time to time in a London flat, where he certainly lived in a bachelor way. And I gave him lunch occasionally at my club. And he was in my own house once or twice, and entertained by my wife, without our ever having a glimmer that there was a Mrs Packford.'

'Two Mrs Packfords, sir. That's rather the point, isn't it?'

'No doubt.' Appleby took another glance at the file. 'The existence of the one easily accounts for his reticence about the other. And vice versa.'

'Just so, sir.'

'I did rather gather that there were ladies somewhere on his horizon, and that he was finding them perplexing. But there isn't, after all, anything uncommon about that. I had a dim feeling that he might be a late beginner, and making heavy weather of it.'

Cavill nodded. 'It's my guess that that was the way of it, sir.'

'But this story you have here' – and Appleby tapped the file – 'is another matter. Crude bigamy just isn't an educated man's crime. He knows it can't be got away with. The thing's nonsense.' Appleby was conscious that his chief reaction to the queer information just presented to him was exasperation. But Packford, he reflected, although so largely sympathetic a character, had always possessed a certain flair for producing that. 'It was when somebody revealed this awkward fact about the dead man,' he went on, 'that the local people asked us to take a look at the business?'

Cavil nodded – still rather wearily. 'That was how it came about, sir.'

'I must say you've lost no time in making up your mind what really happened.' Appleby paused, seeing that Cavill was now smiling faintly. 'But of course I'm still in the dark.' He shook his head rather helplessly – being aware that the spectacle of his chief in some bewilderment would in all probability put Cavill into a better humour. 'Apart from some obscure mutterings when I last ran into him. I'd never connected Packford with that sort of thing.'

'You wouldn't have said, sir, that he was of an enthusiastic temperament?'

'Indeed I should. He was decidedly that.'

'And sanguine? Constitutionally convinced that things would always turn out all right?'

Appleby nodded. 'That too. I see you have formed a very good impression of him, Cavill.'

'Then I don't think it's all quite so much out of the way as we might suppose. There's a type of middle-aged man, you know, who's just the kind of late starter we were talking about. He's been firmly convinced all his days that he's a born bachelor. It's something he's likely to be uneasy about, and you often find it going along with a rather secretive disposition.'

'Packford had that – in a way. But it mostly connected itself with his work. As a man, he usually gave an impression of candour. He wouldn't conceal his delights and triumphs.'

'No doubt, sir. But I think our picture of him is building up very nicely.' Cavill was now entirely happy. Psychological types were his great stand-by and he loved expounding them. A few minutes before, he had ignored an invitation to sit down. But now he tumbled into a chair and wagged a cheerfully egalitarian finger at the Assistant Commissioner. 'One day this type of chap discovers that his doubts and distrusts of himself – in the matter of sex, that's to say – are all moonshine, and that he's been treating himself as an outsider for no good reason at all. It's a discovery that will be very likely to throw him a bit off his balance. He decides that there's nothing in the world to compete with the very simplest tumbling in the hay.'

Appleby smiled. 'Your image doesn't express the matter with much delicacy. But I follow you.'

'And there's almost no folly that such a man, more or less in the first flush of his discovery, won't unhesitatingly commit. He'll take a couple of girls in his stride.'

'I admit that. And I'll even agree that the man might conceivably be Lewis Packford. But surely, my dear fellow, he needn't *marry* them both.'

'He might possibly think it more correct – fairer all round.' Cavill had offered this with every appearance of a serious contribution to the discussion. And Appleby himself saw that, fantastic as it might seem, Packford's mind could really have worked that way. 'And the ladies were unaware of each other's existence?' he asked.

'Certainly they were – just as the rest of Packford's acquaintance was unaware of the existence of either of them. I have a feeling that the whole crazy and dangerous proceeding was very much to the man's taste. It answered to his love of secrecy, and he probably enjoyed laughing up his sleeve about it.'

'Laughing up his sleeve?' It was a phrase, Appleby recalled, that had somehow turned up during his own last conversation with Packford. 'Well, it certainly wasn't a secret that he could have any rational hope of keeping indefinitely. Bluntly put, our eminent scholar was heading for gaol.'

'Of course he was. And as for the ladies, sir, they had in fact just found out. And they had turned up to have the matter out with Packford. That was the precipitating occasion of his suicide.'

Appleby was silent for a moment. 'It takes some believing, you know. It was only an hour ago that I was talking to Packford's solicitor, a fellow called Rood – '

'Ah, Rood,' Cavill spoke tartly. 'I know *him*.'

'Well, Rood said nothing of all this. I can't believe he knows anything about it. And yet he strikes me as a thoroughly acute man.' Appleby shook his head. 'And I still find it uncommonly difficult to think of Packford in this sort of context at all. He was a scholar, Cavill. When I saw him in Italy I'm quite sure that he was utterly absorbed in some plan for discovering whether Shakespeare had ever been there – or at least a project of that kind. There was certainly something else just tugging at his mind. But it's a bit stiff to believe it was a superfluity of wives.'

'I've no doubt, sir, that he was able to leave that behind him in England – at least to some extent. It may even have been his motive for spending the summer in Italy – rather unobtrusively, as I gather it was. His rapturous experiences were over, and he was only anxious that neither of the ladies should come up with him.'

Appleby shrugged his shoulders. 'I can only say, Cavill, that I've seen some queer things in my time. But this is about the queerest.'

'Well, now, that was my feeling about Urchins.'

'Urchins?'

'Packford's house in the country. I suppose it belongs to his brother now.'

'Packford had a brother?'

'A younger brother called Edward. A bit of an eccentric, too, it seems to me. Insisting, for instance, that all those professors and so forth should stop on. Scarcely decent, after such a death. Particularly with the two wives having turned up. Craziest place in England at the moment, I say. But you can take it from me, sir, that there hasn't been a murder.'

'That's not this fellow Rood's opinion. He has a story about Packford having acquired something important from an impoverished nobleman of Ver – '

'Yes, sir, I know all about that.' Cavill's interruption was at once highly improper and an indication that he was now viewing Appleby from a mood of sunny tolerance. 'I think, perhaps, you ought to look at page two.'

Appleby picked up the file again and looked at page two. There was rather a long silence. Page two recorded that Lewis Packford had left a written paper which had been found beside his body. It had been scrawled on a postcard, and read simply:

Farewell, a long farewell!

Appleby stared at this. 'You know that it's a quotation?' he asked. 'Yes, sir. I looked it up.'

'*Farewell, a long farewell, to all my greatness.* It's rather a magniloquent last message to be left even by quite a well-known scholar, isn't it? But he was always quoting Shakespeare, and in a hit-or-miss way.' Appleby looked up at Cavill, frowning. 'It's his writing? I'd have said it was – so far as my memory goes.'

Cavill nodded. 'It's his writing, all right. We've had two experts on it. Only your friend Rood, sir, declares it to be a forgery. Quite nasty about it, he was. Dignity injured. A touchy type. Claims to be a bit of an expert himself.'

'And when you disregarded him, he tackled me. But he didn't tell me about all this.' Appleby pointed to the file again. 'You say the scrawl reproduced here was lying beside the body?'

'Just that.'

'Do you see any significance in the fact that it was written on a postcard?'

'Well, sir, it's certainly a point worth pausing over. But I simply take it that a postcard was the first thing that came handy on his desk.'

'There was other stationery there too?'

'Certainly there was. Packford shot himself in his library, just like one of those baronets in a novel. And this postcard, and his fountain-pen, were lying on the desk.'

Appleby got up, walked to a window, and stared out at the London dusk. '*Farewell, a long farewell,*' he murmured. '*Farewell, a long farewell, to all my greatness.*' He turned and looked sharply at Cavill. 'Has it occurred to you that what Packford wrote on that postcard was no more than a flowery way of saying *any* sort of goodbye? He was always – as I say – spouting Shakespeare. He may well have had the trick of regularly scribbling him too. Has it occurred to you that what we have here is something he might conceivably scrawl on some perfectly trivial and entirely innocent occasion?'

'As far as an intention to commit suicide goes, the words are certainly not very explicit.' Cavill's body had stiffened in his chair as he gave this evasive answer, and Appleby realized that he was angry again. 'They might, of course, be about something quite different. By jove, sir, what a subtle thought.'

'Sorry,' Appleby said. 'Idiotic of me.'

'Well, sir, I'm bound to say I did consider the point you raise. Old fragments of writing have been used in misleading contexts before now. I remember' – Cavill smiled faintly – 'your mentioning it in a lecture.'

'Well, then – how do you meet the point?'

'By believing the testimony of Packford's housekeeper, who seems a perfectly respectable and reliable woman. It was she who heard the shot, and who ran to the library. Packford was slumped over his desk, and the postcard was on his writing-pad. The woman took a good straight look at it. And the ink was wet.'

Appleby took a long breath. 'I don't know much about your literature of baronets in libraries,' he said. 'But my guess is that you might search in vain for just that.'

But Cavill was unimpressed by this sally. 'The point is this, sir,' he said a shade didactically. 'We have a confluence of improbabilities. That this scrawl of Packford's is *not* Packford's is an improbability, since we have the opinion of two of our own experts to set over against the opinion of Rood, who is a mere crank. That the scrawl does *not* refer to his intention of taking his own life is a second improbability, much more likely to turn up in fiction than in fact. And that the respectable woman I have mentioned should be either mistaken or telling a blank lie is a third improbability. All this adds up, surely, to a very big improbability indeed.'

'But Packford's bigamy is as big an improbability as any, my dear Cavill. And yet it is admittedly gospel. So we are reminded that highly improbable things do sometimes occur.'

'That's quite true, sir,' Cavill – perhaps because he felt that he had really established his case – was now entirely patient. 'And you'd find Urchins – if you went down there – pretty hard to believe in at the moment. But there it is. It's a fact. And I'm not arguing that wildly improbable interpretations of evidence are not occasionally vindicated. But I am saying that this Packford business holds no further surprises. What they do about the dead man's two wives and so forth is no business of ours – unless it becomes a question of whether the more recent of them knew what she was about. But that isn't going to interest you or me.'

'I agree with you there.' Appleby had turned back to the window. 'What was that you said about a collection of professors and such like?'

'There was a sort of house-party, sir. People interested in Packford's scholarly discoveries and so forth all gathered there by his invitation. That was the set-up when the thing happened. And Edward Packford has persuaded them to stay on for a little. The whole circus is there now.'

'How very queer.' Appleby had turned round again. 'Cavill – you are sure the affair is closed? I mean – well, a fellow couldn't go down and have another look?'

Cavill stood up and laughed. He laughed at the Assistant Commissioner with a pure affection that went to Appleby's heart. It was one of those moments which, in a rather brittle, rather edgy organization, are worth living for. Then he picked up the file and placed it neatly in the centre of Appleby's desk.

'Good hunting, sir,' Cavill said. And he went out of the room still laughing.

3

Neither Edward Packford nor the local police, when contacted by telephone, took any exception to the idea of further investigation. So Appleby went down by train next day – an antique mode of conveyance across England's smaller distances for which he had a weakness that frequently cost him quite a lot of time. He changed trains at Sherborne and again at Little Urchins. When he got out at Deep Urchins a car was waiting for him. It seemed much as if he were paying the surviving Packfords a purely social visit.

The car was old and lethargic; the woman driving it appeared young and extremely brisk. She could hardly be the respectable housekeeper who figured among Cavill's witnesses, so Appleby put her down as a secretary. She wasted no words, and they drove out of the little station yard in what looked like the beginnings of an oppressive silence. Although the young woman was, so to speak, at the receiving end of the encounter, and thus to be regarded as in possession of the initiative, Appleby thought that she was perhaps waiting until spoken to. Some secretaries were like that. Some were not.

'A queer name,' Appleby hazarded. 'Deep Urchins, I mean.'

'Poor Seth,' the young woman said decisively.

'I beg your pardon?'

The young woman took her eye from the road for a moment – she appeared to be unfamiliar with the car, which felt as if it might be a little unreliable in point of steering mechanism – and looked at

Appleby in sharp appraisal. 'I suppose you know,' she said, 'that Deep Urchins is Thomas Horscroft's Nether Ladds?'

'No. I'm afraid I don't. But the circumstance is, of course, extremely interesting.' Appleby was doing his best. 'And I think you said something about Seth?'

'Poor Seth Cowmeadow, who drowned himself in the pond at Nether Ladds, after letting himself get drunk at the "Welcome Home" and so failing to prevent the boar from eating his grandchild in its cradle.'

'The boar's grandchild?'

'Seth Cowmeadow's grandchild. But I see you haven't read the book.' The young woman took another – and this time frankly disapproving – glance at Appleby.

'I'm afraid I haven't.'

'Professor Quelch of Princeton has just published an absorbingly interesting study of Horscroft's public-houses. Of their names, that is to say. They prove to be deeply meaningful. The "Welcome Home," for example. The name harbours a profound irony.'

'I'm sure it does,' Appleby said. The young woman, he now supposed, must be one of the learned members of the late Lewis Packford's still lingering house-party. Her interest appeared to lie not quite in the dead man's period. But perhaps she ran Shakespeare as a second string.

The car was now running through a hamlet which a signpost announced as Urchin Pydell. The young woman took a hand from the wheel and pointed at a displeasing hovel beyond a ditch. 'The Hangman's Cottage,' she said. 'You remember how –'

'It ought to be condemned,' Appleby said firmly. 'A demolition order, or whatever it's called, from the local authority. Either that, or a shilling charged to literary pilgrims at the door.' He paused. 'And we can't be far from Gaffer's Grave.'

'Gaffer's Grave?'

'Poor Isaac,' Appleby said.

'I don't think I know about that.' The young woman gave Appleby a glance of some suspicion.

'Ah.' Appleby found his invention failing him. 'Did you go up to Lewis Packford's funeral?' he asked rather abruptly. 'I'm not quite clear why it was in London.'

'Something about a family grave. And only his brother Edward went. I didn't. It would have been awkward. If, I mean, we had *both* gone.'

Appleby was puzzled. 'You and his brother?'

'No, no. Myself and this Alice woman. Of course, we could have tossed for it. But it didn't seem quite reverent.'

'I see.' And Appleby did see. He realized, that is to say, that this was one of the two ladies with some claim to be called Mrs Packford. And the Alice woman must be the other. 'Do I understand,' he asked steadily, 'that you and this Alice woman were both at Urchins when your – when Packford died?'

The young woman nodded briskly over the wheel. 'Yes. You see, we had both got wind of Lewis' disgraceful behaviour simultaneously.'

'Got wind of it? You mean, it wasn't a matter of his confessing what he'd done? It had somehow leaked out?'

'This woman and I received anonymous letters by the same post. And we both went straight to Urchins at once.'

'I wonder if you realize,' Appleby said, 'what a lot of explaining this extraordinary situation seems to require? Who is this Alice woman, anyway?'

'I haven't the slightest idea, Sir John.'

'I find that rather hard to believe.' Appleby spoke patiently but with firmness. 'Even if you had never heard of her before the last few days, you have shared with her since then, it seems, a most shocking and harrowing experience. You must have found out something about her. Does she belong to the learned classes – with a line on Thomas Horscroft's Nether Ladds, and Seth Cowmeadow, and all that?'

The young woman driving Appleby gave a hollow laugh. 'She might have a line on the "Welcome Home." I understand Alice is a barmaid.'

'I see. Well, it's a perfectly respectable calling. Would you say that she is simple-minded?'

'Entirely so.'

'Then, if I may say so, she is much the less puzzling of the two of you. May I, by the way, ask your name?'

'You ought to call me Mrs Packford.'

'But at the moment I can't tell – can I? – whether that would be quite fair to Alice. I think you'd better give me your Christian name. Only, of course, for the purposes of ready identification and convenience in internal monologue. It looks as if I shall be doing quite a lot of internal monologuising over this affair. Aloud, I shall call you madam.'

'My name is Ruth.' The young woman had thrown the engine out of gear and was bringing the car to a halt. They were in a deserted lane between high hedges. She had presumably decided that some more leisured conference was desirable before introducing Appleby to Urchins. 'Aren't you striking,' she asked, 'rather a frivolous note? After all, poor Lewis died only – '

'I'm very sorry, I'm sure.' Appleby was sincerely apologetic. 'It's only, you know, that I don't want to strike a note that's all too uncomfortably grim.'

Ruth edged herself sideways in the driving-seat at this and gave him a rather uncertain glance. She wasn't after all, he noticed, exactly young. And she wasn't fast, and she wasn't stupid, and she wasn't – superficially, at least – emotional. In fact, she was quite a problem. 'Grim?' she now asked. 'I'd supposed that, although there's still quite a bit of a mess lying around, the real grimness was over.'

'Perhaps it is, in a way.' Appleby wondered if Ruth was really rather a hard type. 'But I think it fair to explain that the case – for it must be called that – is by no means closed. For instance, Lewis Packford's solicitor – who is not in the least a fool – is disposed to believe that his client was murdered. He has, I'm bound to admit, a very queer notion of why the crime was committed. But his actual suspicion mustn't be accounted negligible.'

Ruth had made no attempt to interrupt this speech, and she remained silent for a further moment now. When she did speak, it was rather surprisingly. 'But it's not possible,' she said. 'You know it's not possible. I wish it was.'

'You wish that Packford had been murdered?'

'Well, yes – in a way.' As she said this, Ruth looked rather bewildered, as if the oddity of the sentiment were coming home to her. 'Because it was unlike him – to kill himself because he'd been a bloody fool.' She paused. 'It's disconcerting, I suppose, to have a person one believes one knows well acting suddenly out of character. Particularly when the action is, at least by conventional standards, a little craven.'

'Or even ridiculous?' Appleby, as he asked this, was conscious that he was quickly coming to have a considerable respect for Ruth. Whether he was coming to have any liking for her was a different matter. And the mere puzzle of her grew. She was too intelligent for her own slightly ludicrous situation to be at all easily explained.

'Or even ridiculous,' she agreed gravely. 'But I don't think, Sir John, that you can have been given all the facts. Lewis left a message saying – '

'We needn't tackle that now,' Appleby said. He was determined to steer this interview his own way. 'But I may say that I've had a pretty full report from an experienced officer of my own.'

'Yes, I think I met him. Mr Cavill.'

'Exactly. And it's fair to say that he agrees with you, madam.'

'But you don't?'

Appleby took a second to answer this. 'I do see,' he said presently, 'some possibility of keeping an open mind.'

Ruth Packford – if it was proper to call her that – had produced a cigarette-case. As she held it out to Appleby he noticed that her fingers were those of a heavy smoker. In spite of her air of brisk competence she was probably one who didn't find life altogether easy. But of the competence there was no doubt. It was instanced in her having taken on the job of meeting Appleby at the railway station.

She must have taken some initiative over that, since she was herself, according to her own account, too recent an arrival at Urchins to make such an assignment a matter of course. Certainly one felt she had never driven this particular old car before. She had presumably possessed herself of it with the object of contriving just this present *tête-à-tête*.

'Of course,' she was saying, 'I'm perfectly willing to be open-minded too. It's the grand condition of all successful research. My work teaches me that.'

Appleby received this respectfully. Ruth, he supposed, was what is called a professional woman – a species sometimes uneasily conscious of amateurishness in some of the normal fields of female activity. She was looking at him slightly defiantly now. 'And you were unaware,' he asked, 'that there was this other person in Lewis Packford's life?'

There was a moment's silence. Appleby was conscious that his question, as phrased, had a somewhat literary ring, so that she might judge she was being made fun of. But she answered at once. 'I hadn't a clue,' she said. 'Is that very queer?'

'I don't know if it's so queer as the fact that nobody seems to have had a clue about *you*. Mr Rood, for instance, who was Packford's solicitor. It seems extraordinary that a man should conceal a marriage from his solicitor.'

'He might well conceal *two*.'

'A man is certainly likely to conceal the fact that he had been so idiotic as to contract a bigamous and invalid marriage. But why conceal the first and valid one?'

Ruth laughed. 'But that, you see, was the one with me. And it was perfectly natural.'

'I assure you it doesn't bear that appearance. Why should you contract a secret marriage with a perfectly respectable and indeed eminent person, and never so much as enter his house?'

She laughed again. 'The explanation is so obvious that I'd expect you to have thought of it,' she said. 'I teach in a women's college, you see. And the conditions of my employment preclude marriage. If it

had been known that I was married, I'd have been obliged to vacate
– I believe that's the word – to vacate my fellowship. And I didn't
want to do that. My work means a great deal to me.'

'You mean that you've been continuing to hold your job under
false pretences? Isn't that going to be rather awkward now?'

'Not in the least. You haven't listened to what I said. The words I
used were "*If it had been known that I was married.*" They precisely
represent the legal situation. You see, our statutes, or whatever they
are called, were drawn up for us by some wicked old judge. And there
are several places, it seems, where he amused himself by inserting
small absurdities that wouldn't be noticed by a pack of guileless
learned women. This is one of them. The relevant clause begins
"*Should it come to the cognizance of the College Council.*" There's no
onus upon any of us, should she get married, to say a word or do
anything. Lewis spotted that.'

'He would.' Appleby said this with conviction.

'And, of course, we didn't cheat about the money. I was still legally
entitled to my salary. But Lewis, who was quite well off, thought it
wouldn't be the thing to take it. So I've been paying it into a trust
fund to found a scholarship.'

'The Lewis Packford Shakespeare Scholarship, no doubt.' Appleby
supposed himself to have said this with marked irony.

'Oh, yes – how clever of you to guess!' Ruth seemed really pleased.
'Lewis decided it should be that.'

'Lewis, if you ask me, decided a great deal. The whole outrageous
scheme of concealment was clearly his.'

'It wasn't outrageous!' Ruth was indignant. 'I've explained to you
how we played entirely fair.'

'There was certainly one person who didn't get fair play – and that
is yourself. And it wasn't long before you had ceased to think it fun,
and were acknowledging to yourself that it was very foolish and
rather humiliating.' Appleby had decided to smack out at Ruth. 'For
instance, your husband going off to a bachelor life on Lake Garda –
where I happened, by the way, to visit him – while you were doing
some learned dreary useless thing at home – lecturing, I shouldn't be

surprised, on the decay of metaphysical poetry to a Summer School for Patagonians.'

'I've never in my life done anything of the kind!' Ruth was extremely indignant. 'You are being quite idiotic and – and improperly flippant and familiar.'

'So I am.' Appleby smiled at her inoffensively. 'But I'm old enough to be your father, and I think I'll put things to you after my own fashion. Packford was a fascinating chap. I liked him very much, or I wouldn't be here now. But he had a mania for secrets and surprises. And he must have got you right under his thumb.'

'Lewis didn't get me under his thumb!' Ruth's indignation grew.

'He must positively have hypnotized you, my dear young lady, or you would never have agreed to so absurd a course of conduct. And you really knew it – although you were repressing the knowledge and persuading yourself that, for a time at least, it was all a great lark. I'm very sorry to speak in this way about your relations with a man you were certainly much in love with, and who is only just dead. It's not very decent. Unfortunately it's my business to go ahead – and rather rapidly, because there are a good many calls upon my time. So what I'm saying is this: you were already in a state of some disillusion and some dissatisfaction when you got this incredible news. One secret marriage had so ticked his irresponsible fancy that he'd promptly gone off and contracted a second with someone called Alice. Unless, of course, Alice really came first. I just haven't heard any evidence bearing on that as yet. But it's not, perhaps, a point of the first importance. What is significant is that you were in a raging fury.'

Ruth lit a second cigarette from the stub of the first. She did it with difficulty, since her hands trembled and she was holding Appleby in a fixed terrified glance. 'What are you saying?' she said. 'I don't understand you.'

'Somebody sent you an anonymous letter, containing what you must have supposed or hoped was a stupid and cruel joke. You hurried to Urchins – and the thing proved to be true. There was this other woman, brought there by a similar message. No doubt she was in a raging fury too. And what happened? Packford couldn't take it.

The situation was beyond him, and he shot himself. There oughtn't, really, to be much difficulty in believing that. Am I right?'

'It sounds reasonable.' She spoke cautiously, doubtingly. It might have been because she was unconvinced, or because she felt obscurely that Appleby was baiting a trap.

'Have you nothing more to say than that? What was in your mind when you seized the initiative, so to speak, this morning – grabbing this car to come and meet me with? Why did it strike you as advantageous to get in first?'

'If it's as a police officer that you are coming to Urchins, I much doubt whether your method of questioning isn't singularly irregular.' Ruth offered this with spirit. And she was now quite calm again. 'It was simply this: if there is to be further investigation, I ought to be heard first. It's due to my position that it should be so. But if I'd simply let you arrive at Urchins, there might have been a stupid scene, with Alice barging to the front.'

'A matter of precedence – I see. By the way, what kind of person would you say this Alice was?'

'Dead vulgar.' Ruth snapped this out. And then at once she added: 'I'd say she wasn't a bad sort.'

'Lewis Packford's taste wouldn't lead him far astray?'

'As far as poetry and that sort of thing is concerned, Lewis' taste simply didn't exist. But I think he'd be not too bad on people.'

Appleby's interest in Ruth grew. He still didn't at all know whether she was positively likeable. But certainly she was formidable, which was a quality he rather liked anyway. 'It would be fair to say,' he asked, 'that you really were two angry women, and that neither of you made any bones about showing it?'

'That's perhaps fair enough. But you mustn't suppose that my feelings are bitter now. Indeed, I don't know that they were ever that. As soon as I'd got control of myself I felt Lewis' actions had been – well, quite understandable. Indeed, it was some quite good qualities that had got him into his jam.'

'I see – or rather I don't.' Appleby paused, awaiting explanations. He had to ask himself, he was acutely aware, whether he was not in the presence of a clever woman rather over-playing her hand. One could readily decide that all this dispassionateness and magnanimity was a little too good to be true.

'He was a boundlessly enthusiastic person. And marriage – which was, of course, quite a late adventure with him – took him decidedly that way. And then we made that foolish decision. Don't think I can't really see it as a foolish decision. And I must insist that it was very much my fault at the time. If I hadn't, I mean, showed that I'd much like to keep my job, then that secretive genius of Lewis' which you seem to know about wouldn't have had this new sphere to exercise itself in. But there it was. And keeping our marriage dark meant a lot of separation – and at a time when Lewis, a middle-aged man new to the whole thing, was in a thoroughly excited state. Sex had taken an entirely novel role in his life. And being sanguine and generous and careless, he was – well, very vulnerable.'

Ruth paused. She was saying all this in a low steady voice which was far from suggesting an insensitive attitude to her subject. 'I can see,' Appleby said cautiously, 'the kind of thing you mean.'

'Before he knew where he was, he was in bed with this girl. It's not gratifying to reflect on, but I suppose it is natural enough.'

'Perhaps so. But there was nothing natural in going through a form of marriage with her.'

'Wasn't there? I doubt whether you know Lewis really well. The girl was on his hands – quite suddenly. He must have felt rather like a cricketer, fielding close in, who becomes aware he's made a catch. He's planned nothing, made no sort of grab, but there the ball is.'

'Very apt,' Appleby said. He spoke a shade dryly. Ruth, he thought, was going out of her way in search of charity.

'There she was, I say. And she wasn't a person with any less real a claim on him simply because she did a little smell, perhaps, of the public bar.' Ruth paused on this – so that it was almost possible to suspect that she had divined the fact that verisimilitude would be furthered by at least the hint of an astringent note. 'And no doubt she revealed herself as artlessly and trustingly inclined to matrimony. In such circumstances, Lewis would certainly judge it a shame not to provide it. So he did.' Ruth paused again. 'And now I think we'll drive on.'

'Yes, drive on.' Appleby watched her throw away her second cigarette and start up the engine of the ancient car. 'But could Packford,' he asked, 'do such a fundamentally muddle-headed and irresponsible thing? He was, after all, a highly intelligent man.'

'It was a canalized sort of intelligence. It all went into a sort of jet propulsion, driving on his work. Outside that, he was capable of any number of ineptitudes.' Ruth's voice had changed, and Appleby's startled ear had to acknowledge that what it now held was tenderness. 'Don't you remember how clumsy he was?'

'Yes, I do.'

'And isn't bigamy about the clumsiest crime a man can commit?' she laughed softly. 'So there you are.'

'It's a crime that may be extremely cruel and heartless. On the other hand, it may be committed in such circumstances as to be not much more than silly.' Appleby paused. 'If one misses out the theological aspect, that is to say.'

'Lewis was certainly being merely silly.' Suddenly, she was almost crying out. 'And it oughtn't – oh, it oughtn't – to have brought him to his death!'

'If it did.'

There was a long silence, unbroken until Ruth had swung the car between rusty iron gates and up a somewhat neglected drive. 'Urchins doesn't exactly flourish,' she said. 'A comfortable sort of semi-decay. Plenty of money for food and books and travel. But beyond that – well, I'm beginning to be doubtful.'

'I see.'

The silence renewed itself. They were in sight of the house before Ruth spoke again. 'Talking of travel,' she said, 'will you tell me something?'

'Certainly – if I can.'

'You said you visited Lewis when he had the villa on Lake Garda. What did he talk about?' She hesitated. 'For instance, did he have anything to say about – ' She hesitated again.

Appleby smiled. 'About you – or even about Alice? No, not a word. There were one or two moments when I found myself speculating as to whether he had involved himself in some personal perplexity. But it wasn't because of anything at all explicit in his conversation.'

'Then, Sir John, what *did* he talk about?'

Appleby had to consider only for a moment. 'Forgery,' he said.

4

Urchins turned out to be a surprisingly large house. It seemed moreover to be of considerable antiquity. But it had been made a mess of, comparatively late in its history, by some owner with a taste for the Gothic. And this must have been done on the cheap, for the battlements, pointed windows and so forth were now in a crumbling and tumbling condition and what remained solid appeared to be of an altogether earlier date. The whole place could only be described as in shocking disrepair.

And it had something to tell, Appleby supposed, about its late owner. Packford could have taken very little interest in this – presumably – ancestral home. Appleby remembered him as only vaguely and conventionally aware of his surroundings at Garda – just conscious that his villa was modest and his summer-house rather grand; gesturing unseeingly at the *grotteschi* from which he believed himself to be experiencing pleasure; boundlessly enthusiastic over the idea of giving masterful instructions to Gino, but not really at all possessed of the difference between one shrub and another. All Packford's real traffic had been with the memorials and signs and traces of things, and not with things in themselves. What was left of things in the library of the British Museum, in the neglected muniment rooms of houses just like this, in the Public Record Office: his real territory had been there. Conceivably the two ladies in the case were the first material objects of which he had ever become aware, so to speak at all vividly in the round.

Yes, Urchins looked decidedly emaciated. Packford, without much noticing the fact, had possibly starved it for years. And so it might well be an inconvenient sort of inheritance now. Probably it went to Edward Packford, and not to whichever of the ladies proved to be the dead man's authentic spouse. In default of a direct heir, places of this sort were commonly tied up that way.

Appleby knew nothing about Edward Packford. But then there was a lot of information which, despite Cavill's rapid conscientious survey of what seemed an unmysterious suicide, he didn't yet possess. And in a way the scent – if there was one – was slightly cold. And yet it appeared that there was one odd – and even perplexing – circumstance that bore the other way. Lewis Packford had been entertaining some kind of house-party at the time of his death. And now, several days later, these people were still at Urchins, presumably as the guests of Edward. It might be a good idea to find out about them at once.

Ruth had drawn up the ancient car before the front door of the house. There was a long shallow porch facing south, and now bathed in warm sunshine. Deck-chairs, tables and a scattering of cushions and books and newspapers struck one note; dandelions sprouting between chinks in the flagstones struck another. Not far away a very old man was rather ineffectively gathering up between two boards a first scattering of the leaves of autumn.

'Do you mind,' Appleby asked, 'if I leave my suitcase in the car, and hope that somebody will give me a lift to a pub afterwards?'

Ruth seemed surprised. 'But Edward will expect you to stop at Urchins. He's very hospitable. For instance, he makes no bones whatever about continuing to house at the moment two sisters-in-law by one brother. Many men would think that a bit steep.'

It seemed to Appleby that Ruth was not without a sense of humour. 'And what about those other people who are continuing to stay on?' he asked. 'Who exactly are they?'

'I think they might be called the members of a sort of club or society – or least of a coterie – to which Lewis belonged. Normally, I gather, they simply dine together three or four times a year. But sometimes Lewis liked to gather them in for a weekend.'

'And I suppose they too are learned?'

'Well, some of them. Scholars, collectors, bibliophiles – a mixed lot. And they indulge a life of fantasy.'

'They do *what*?' Appleby was puzzled.

'It's a species of literary joke about an imaginary eighteenth-century antiquarian called Bogdown. They read each other papers about him. Transactions of the Bogdown Society. That sort of thing. I expect it's great fun.'

'It sounds uproarious.' Appleby couldn't be sure whether Ruth's judgement on this singular diversion was, or was not, ironically intended. 'But you've never been let in on it?'

'Of course not. It's entirely for men. And there's one of them now, coming out of the front door. Professor Prodger.'

'The old person with the white beard?'

'Yes. He's terribly eminent. And he's tracing Bogdown's books. They were dispersed, you see, at the Bogdown sale in 1784. At least I think it was 1784.'

'Is that why Prodger is eminent?'

'Of course not. Haven't I explained that Bogdown is just a game? Prodger's serious work is on the development of the comic Irishman in English drama.'

'Oh.'

'You'd better meet him now, while I go and find Edward.'

They had got out of the car, and Ruth led the way up to Professor Prodger, who had settled down in a deck-chair. She performed a perfunctory introduction, and then vanished. Appleby had an idea that she proposed making some sort of report to their host before confronting him with the new visitor.

The professor had got to his feet in order to shake hands, and this had involved him in dropping his glasses, the case in which he carried them, a newspaper and a couple of books. When Appleby had helped to recover these, the two men sat down. 'I'm afraid,' Prodger said mildly and from behind his beard, 'that I know very little about your kind of thing – very little indeed. But I have a good Eliot and Chapman which I should be delighted to show you one day, and also a Derome that's quite a pleasure to handle.'

'Thank you very much.' Appleby's professional preoccupations prompted him to suppose for a moment that Prodger was a collector of little-known fire-arms. 'I don't think I've ever seen a Derome.'

This reply plainly prompted thought. 'Am I not to understand,' Prodger presently asked with a courteous inclination of his venerable head, 'that I am addressing Dr Appleby, the distinguished student of bibliopegy?'

Appleby, although hazy about bibliopegy, was quite certain he wasn't a distinguished student of it. 'No. I'm afraid you must have taken me for somebody else.'

'No matter, no matter. In fact I am rather glad to hear it. The history of bookbinding is a trivial sort of lore, after all. An amusement for collectors, sir. And we know what *they* are like. Eh?' Prodger had a high faint senile laugh. 'But no doubt you have come down to Urchins because you have some interest in the mystery? We all have. That is why we are staying on, you know – that is why we are staying on. And I must warn you, Dr Appleby, that we are a mixed lot. Poor Packford was not always very careful about his associations and – um – practices.'

'I'm very sorry to hear it.' Appleby supposed this to be a reference to the dead man's unfortunate matrimonial adventures.

'Limbrick and Rixon, for instance. They are both here, I am sorry to say. Limbrick, of course, is the well-known collector, and we know what *that* means. Eh?' Prodger repeated his laugh. It was the sort of noise one associates with agitated guinea-pigs. 'And Canon Rixon is Librarian to the Chapter at Barchester. At least I think it is Barchester. But there is no doubt as to his occupation. I have always found it to be one conducing to a singular depravity both of intellect and morals. And I am confident you agree with me. There may be meritorious exceptions. But as a class of persons they are wholly to be deplored.'

'Cathedral librarians?' It seemed to Appleby that it would be hard to think up a more blameless walk of life.

'Certainly, certainly.' Prodger's beard could be seen as quivering with indignation. 'I have never found one yet who is interested in low comedy in the Anglo-Irish theatre. Men utterly devoid of the instinct of scholarship, Dr Appleby. Not, of course, that they are as bad as wealthy collectors.'

'You would say that wealthy collectors are very bad?'

'They will buy anything, you know, and sit on it. Limbrick is sitting at this moment on the broken plough.'

'Isn't that very uncomfortable?' Appleby was becoming rather dazed.

'*The Broken Plough* is Thomas Horscroft's last work, existing only in a single manuscript now owned by Limbrick. We have with us, by the way, quite an authority on Horscroft's books – a young woman who turned up, for some reason, a few days ago.'

'Yes. She has just introduced me to you. She says she is Lewis Packford's widow.'

'Is that so?' Prodger appeared to take no interest in this topic. 'Now, what was I saying? Ah, yes – collectors. Limbrick is bad enough. But consider that fellow in New York – or is it Chicago?'

'I'm afraid I don't know.'

'Sankey – is that his name? In a much bigger way than Limbrick. Buys anything on any terms, you know, however flagrantly dishonest. And then sits on it. But all collectors are like that. Deny you access to their most important materials – and simply to aggrandize themselves in their own eyes. Worse than the monks in their cathedrals. *They* used to chain up their books, you know, chain up their books. And I am accustomed to say that the wealthy modern collectors still have the chained-book mentality.'

Professor Prodger paused as if to let laughter subside; this must have been a quip he was accustomed to offer his students. Appleby took the opportunity to get in a word. 'What do you think about the mystery yourself?' he asked.

'It was almost certainly another of Packford's Shakespeare discoveries, I should say. And something quite big. Important new light, perhaps, on the chronology of the plays. Or information on how Shakespeare was occupied during his twenties. There are nearly ten blank years to fill in, you know – nearly ten blank years.'

'Packford was hinting he was on to something big?'

'Certainly. It was no doubt the occasion of his bringing us together. He liked to work up excitement, poor fellow, by dropping a word here and there.'

'I've already gathered there was something of the sort in the wind.' Appleby paused. Edward Packford, he was thinking, was taking rather a long time to appear. 'But when you spoke of the mystery, Professor, I thought you were referring to the circumstances of Packford's death. Would you judge them to be mysterious?'

'He is said to have shot himself, poor fellow. But I suspect foul play, Dr Appleby. One must expect trouble, surely, if one has shady characters about the place.'

'Shady characters?'

'Certainly. Limbrick and Canon Rixon, you know. It is true that they have been members, more or less, of our small informal group for some time. But it is a different matter having them under one's own roof – eh? It is very clear, to my mind, where the finger of suspicion points.'

'You suspect one of these two – Limbrick or Rixon – of having murdered Packford?'

'Both of them, I should say. I would not care to settle the proportion of iniquity between them.'

'This is a very grave suggestion, Professor Prodger.' Appleby didn't manage to speak with much conviction. It seemed impossible not to conclude that this old person was merely raving. There had been force in Cavill's implication that he would find a mild madness pervasive at Urchins.

'As a matter of fact, we have had the police here. They began, very properly, to make inquiries. But they seem to have gone away again.'

'If it's any satisfaction to you, they're back.' Appleby said this firmly. 'I'm a policeman myself.'

'You astonish me, my dear sir.' Prodger said this not at all like a man who is astonished. 'I understood you to say that you were a student of bibliopegy. But no matter. Ah, here is our host.'

Appleby rose from his chair and turned to meet Edward Packford. And for a moment he experienced a species of confusion which he found it hard to account for. It was like being unexpectedly confronted with a disturbing ocular phenomenon. Edward Packford seemed to exist in some abnormal relationship with physical space, like a figure set by a primitive painter in an imperfectly organized perspective scene. But in another second the explanation of all this turned out to be quite simple. Edward was an almost exact miniature reproduction of his dead brother. He had the same features, the same chunky proportions, and the same way of carrying himself. But he was quite small. So he presented himself to Appleby's vision as farther off than the available space permitted.

'How do you do?' Edward advanced and shook hands. He even had Lewis Packford's rather clumsy movements and scattered manner. But he had quite a different eye. It was keen and briskly purposive – the eye, Appleby told himself, of a man ruled by the practical intellect. And he certainly wasn't under the illusion that his visitor dealt in bibliopegy. 'I am very glad you have come down,' he said. 'I am far from satisfied about the manner of Lewis' death.' He turned to Prodger. 'Sherry in the library, Professor.'

'Ah! There is much to be said for that. There is much to be said for a glass of sherry before lunch.' And Prodger, with only a slight delay occasioned by his again dropping his books and glasses, toddled obediently off. Appleby wondered why Edward Packford, who could briskly dismiss a guest this way, should have continued to entertain at

Urchins a number of his brother's acquaintances who might much more properly have taken themselves off.

But an answer to this, as it happened, turned up at once. 'You will find everybody here,' Edward said, 'who was staying with Lewis when he died. I persuaded them to stay on for a little, even after the police and so forth appeared to have lost interest in us. I had a notion, you see, that the interest might revive again. And I was right – for here you are.'

'Here I am – if you will bear with me.' As Appleby expressed himself in this amiably unofficial way he continued to size Edward up. He was a man entirely composed and sure of himself; and if his manner was somewhat sombre and reserved, that was natural enough in one who had just lost a brother in circumstances such as the present. Certainly he had every appearance of owning both the will and ability to go straight to the point; and after the maunderings of Professor Prodger this came to Appleby as something of a relief. 'Mr Packford,' he said, 'may I ask you at once why you are not satisfied with what are at least the surface indications in this sad business?'

'It wasn't like Lewis.' Edward waved Appleby into a chair, sat down himself, and then leant forward in an attitude that emphasised the forthright quality of his words. 'It was damned unlike him. I can't see him blowing his own brains out, even if things were going dead against him. And they weren't. On the contrary, everything was coming his way.'

'I seem to have gathered that it was two wives that were coming his way. Wouldn't you be inclined to admit that as a somewhat adverse circumstance, Mr Packford?'

'It was a thoroughly queer one, anyway. And of course Lewis had been almost unbelievably foolish. But the thing isn't utterly out of character, as taking his own life because of such a scrape would be.'

'Were you yourself aware that he had committed bigamy?'

'Yes and no, Sir John. That's to say, Lewis had told me about the situation, but I hadn't quite managed to believe it. That sounds silly.

But I really had a vague feeling that he was exaggerating. He was given to exaggeration.'

'You mean that you doubted whether he had really gone through what purported to be a legal form of marriage with this person called Alice, and thus brought himself within the reach of the law?'

'Just that. I suspected some freakish and – no doubt – highly reprehensible joke or mummery by which this girl had been taken in after a fashion he honestly hadn't intended her to be. Something like that. I saw the situation vaguely as a scrape. And I strongly advised him to take discreet legal advice. Whether he did or not, I don't know. The next thing was that each of these women was tipped off about the situation.'

Appleby nodded. 'So I've gathered. They received anonymous letters, and down they both came to Urchins?'

'Just that. And then my brother was found dead, with this note beside him. It all looks like cause and effect, but I'm not happy about it.'

'I think I can understand that.' Appleby was silent for a moment. 'Do I understand that you were at Urchins yourself when your brother died?'

'I wish I had been. I might have been quite good at summary justice.' Edward flashed this out with a sudden odd fire that set Appleby wondering. 'But in point of fact I was in Paris on business, and had to fly back as soon as I got the news. No – there were only his housekeeper and servants, the two ladies who had arrived so disconcertingly, and this queer collection of Lewis' precious cronies.'

'I see.' Appleby smiled. 'Would I be right in guessing that you didn't much share your brother's interests, and that all these people aren't your sort of crowd?'

'Certainly you're right. I had a great regard for the distinction Lewis had gained, and I've no doubt that Prodger and the rest of them are extremely learned. But I'm no antiquarian myself.'

'Apart from his little matrimonial problem, you're not aware that your brother had any serious worries?'

Edward frowned. 'I begin to think he might have had a bit of a headache over money – if he was capable of turning his attention to it. I'll know more about that when his solicitor – a fellow called Rood – comes down with the will and so forth this evening. But it's already my guess that things aren't in a particularly good way.'

'Your brother wasn't much of a business man?'

'Far from it. The truth is, Sir John, that there was a streak of irresponsibility running right through Lewis. It emerges startlingly in this matter of his first treating himself to a secret marriage and then – as if that wasn't enough – adding a dash of bigamy.'

'I suppose there's no doubt that the lady called Ruth is the legal wife, and the other the bigamous one?'

Edward shook his head. 'No doubt at all, I'd say. Mind you, I don't altogether blame Lewis over Alice. She's more my idea of a wife.'

'I haven't met Alice yet. But I don't think too badly of Ruth.' Appleby smiled. 'Not that she'd be altogether my idea of a wife either.'

'Ruth comes out of Lewis' own stable. She's a lady professor, you know. I've no doubt it was that sort of community of interests that gave Lewis the courage to make up to her in the first place. He was always damned shy of women. Believed they weren't at all his cup of tea. But once he'd got going with Ruth he changed his mind. He liked women after all. He even discovered that he liked them best without professorial trimmings. The quintessential female was just his line – and it had taken him all those years to discover it. So when you see Alice you'll agree it was natural that he should be knocked sideways.'

'Such things happen, no doubt.' Appleby was noncommittal. Edward's attitude to his late brother seemed decidedly indulgent – whereas, actually, Lewis Packford's conduct appeared worse the more carefully one looked at it. The notion that he had, so to speak, graduated from Ruth to Alice wasn't pretty. And if Ruth herself had reason to see it in that light then it was almost inconceivable that her present appearance of charity in the whole matter was not in large measure assumed. Buried somewhere in her there must be a very different emotion.

Edward Packford was looking at his watch – with a gesture which precisely reminded Appleby of his brother's doing the same thing in his summer-house on Garth. 'Look here,' Edward said, 'we've time for a drink before lunch. But not, I'd suggest, with that crowd. I'm beginning to feel I've seen enough of them, and you can open your own innings over the cutlets. Come along to my small room.'

They entered the house and went down a long corridor with a vaulted ceiling. It appeared that parts of the interior had been transformed to suit the Gothic taste too. 'I had this as a boy,' Edward said as he threw open a door, 'and Lewis always insisted that I should hang on to it. Not that I used it much when I was down here. For Lewis and I, you know, although our interests weren't much in common, suffered each other's company tolerably well.' Edward was silent for a moment, and Appleby was aware that he had heard – perhaps, that he had been intended to hear – a careful understatement. And then at once his host walked over to a table and poured drinks, while Appleby glanced around the room. It was still essentially a schoolboy's, with shabby books piled on the shelves, and colour prints and House photographs on the walls, and on the chimney-piece a mangy stuffed badger in a cracked glass case.

Edward pointed familiarly to a chair. 'I know you're not here to answer questions,' he said. 'But perhaps you'll just tell me whether, in your opinion, there can really be anything in my feeling that we're far from having got at the truth about Lewis' death?'

'There would have been no point in my coming down, Mr Packford, if I'd judged the matter closed.'

Edward nodded, and gave what sounded like a satisfied grunt. 'But there was that damned postcard. Of course you'll have heard about it. Is there any getting round it?'

'I don't want precisely to get round it. But I do want to give it a good deal of thought. You judged it to be certainly in your brother's handwriting?'

'Decidedly I did. But I'm no expert.'

'Experts have agreed with you, it appears. Not that their opinion absolutely settles such a point. Tip-top forgers aren't all that easily detected within the compass of a few scrawled words.'

'So I'd suppose, Sir John. But the presence of such a person in the affair is rather an extravagant idea to start with. And then there's the astonishing fact that Mrs Husbands, the housekeeper, actually observed the ink not yet dry on the card.'

'Mrs Husbands might be imagining that. She satisfied my chap Cavill as reliable, I admit. But she is reporting on something which she thought she saw at a moment of terrific shock. And I assure you that people who appear entirely well-balanced may swear to the queerest things in such circumstances. Or again, this Mrs Husbands may be lying.' Appleby paused. 'But take the first possibility, and suppose that she was simply mistaken about the ink. And suppose at the same time that the writing is genuinely your brother's. Is it particularly impressive evidence – evidence that is anything like conclusive?'

'I don't think it is – not in the circumstances. My brother, bless him, was always peddling Shakespeare. He was quite capable of sending off a postcard like that in half-a-dozen different situations – say to an unsatisfactory tradesman with whom he didn't mean to deal again. *Farewell, a long farewell.*' Edward's voice had dropped, as if he were carefully controlling it. 'I can just hear Lewis roaring with laughter at what he would consider an extremely good joke.' He raised his glass and gazed into it sombrely. 'But if Mrs Husbands is neither lying nor mistaken? Then we must accept it that Lewis – ?' Edward left his question unfinished.

'I'm not at all sure that we must. But it's not, if you will forgive me, a conjecture I want to take much farther at the moment. For a start, Mr Packford, I want to see the library – and Mrs Husbands.'

'Prodger and his crew are in the library now. Perhaps after lunch – '

But Appleby shook his head. 'If you don't mind,' he said, 'I'll defer the business of meeting the rest of your house-party. Get them into lunch, then get me into the library. And then – yes, get this Mrs Husbands to bring me something there on a tray.'

'But, dash it all, you haven't come, my dear sir, to tinker with the clocks or tune the piano!' Edward Packford's sense of hospitable fitness was clearly disturbed.

'I probably haven't come to do anything so agreeable.' Appleby had stood up, suddenly grim. 'When I enter a house in the way of my profession, it would often be tolerably accurate to describe me as the man who has come about the drains.'

Edward Packford too had got to his feet. 'Unsavoury excavations?' he asked. 'Well, that's fair warning. And I can only say that I hope you will go through with them.'

5

The room in which Appleby presently found himself had clearly been a library for a long time. Eighteenth-century Packfords had doubtless here surveyed with complacency their undisturbed rows of handsomely tooled and gilded leather. There was still a mass of stuff to delight any authentic student of bibliopegy who should be set browsing in the place; Eliot and Chapman – to say nothing of Derome – were almost certainly well represented. But in addition to being the sort of library that many country houses can show, this room was also the workshop of a scholar. One table held a litter of photostats; another, piles of unbound learned journals. Here and there drawers and filing-cabinets gaped open – having been stuffed with papers until they could no longer perform their designed functions. Some raw shelving had been run up at one end to stack additional books – most of which seemed older than those more handsomely accommodated. There was a smell of leather.

Lewis Packford had worked here, and here he had died. Appleby walked to the large desk that stood almost in the middle of the room and studied it thoughtfully. It was quite bare, and he knew that its whole surface had been tested for fingerprints. So had everything that had previously been standing on it; there was a careful list in Cavill's file. There was a modern, well-upholstered revolving chair before the desk. Packford had died in this. Appleby sat down on it.

A man sitting thus, and thus blowing out his brains, would slump forward, so. Of course the body had been moved before any police officer set eyes on it; only in romances are the common instincts of humanity set in abeyance on such occasions. They had lifted the poor chap on that couch. But he had been unmistakably dead.

From his briefcase Appleby produced Cavill's notes. The revolver was one which nobody had owned to ever seeing before. But it was a common Army type, and it is only in romances, again, that such things are traceable. It had been lying on the floor – and Lewis Packford's hand had certainly held it. But had that hand belonged to a living man, or to a dead one? When a man is thus shot at very close range, only an eye-witness can positively exclude murder. Unless, of course, the conditions are such that no murderer could have got away.

And that – Appleby said to himself as he stood up again and walked round the room – certainly doesn't apply in this case. Here is the door through which Mrs Husbands entered, having had to come some distance after hearing the shot. And there is the second door, leading to what is virtually a deserted wing of this rambling house. And there again, straight in front of the desk, is a French window giving on a terrace. And there, yet again, in a corner of the lofty room, stands a cast-iron spiral staircase to a light gallery giving access to the highest ranges of books – and off which, apparently, a small door, concealed by sham books, opens direct upon a higher storey on that side of the house. The whole affords an excellent setting not merely for homicide but even for complicated farce, with actors popping divertingly in and out all over the place.

And there had, after all, been scope for something like farce – or at least for domestic comedy – at Urchins on that night last week when Packford had died. Professor Prodger would obviously be a great success in any absurd play. And Lewis Packford himself had contrived a situation which could be exhibited as entirely ludicrous. But what had actually happened was of another order of drama.

Appleby looked at the window-curtains. They were of a very heavy stuff. He turned on the electric lights, and then drew the curtains across their windows, one by one. He produced his pocket-book, and from his pocket-book a postcard. It was the original postcard – the crux of the whole affair. *Farewell, a long farewell...* He tossed it on the desk, and studied it now from one angle and now from another. He did this with all the lights on, with some of the lights on, with only a single desk-light on. It was this last effect which he was considering when there was a cry and a crash behind him. He turned round. A handsome woman – presumably Mrs Husbands – was standing transfixed in the open doorway. And there was a tray and a litter of broken china on the floor.

This disaster didn't take very long to sort out, so that it had to be concluded that Mrs Husbands was a competent woman. And it wasn't until she had set a fresh and undisturbed tray before Appleby that she spoke. 'Was it necessary,' she asked coldly, 'to stage that crude theatrical effect?'

'You are quite mistaken, madam. I am afraid I had entirely forgotten that you would be coming into the library. Nothing was farther from my thoughts than to distress you in any way. Please accept my apologies.'

'Thank you.' Mrs Husbands received these protestations with the scepticism they conceivably deserved. 'I am glad it was not one of the servants. I hear nothing from them now but that this or that has given them, as they say, quite a turn. And I admit that you gave that to me. The scene was a little too close to what I came upon last week. No doubt it is what you call a reconstruction of the crime.'

'The crime?'

'Suicide is a crime, I have been told.'

'No doubt. But all that I was in fact attempting to reconstruct was the appearance which that postcard probably bore when you first saw it. And you can guess what I am after, Mrs Husbands. I want to see whether, in one light or another, some gleam or glitter from its surface might suggest wet ink.'

'How very ingenious. But the ink was in simple fact wet.'

Appleby bowed. 'I am far from being disposed to question the veracity of your evidence in the matter. It satisfied, as you will remember, a thoroughly capable officer of my own. But in a crisis, you know, one can sometimes form – perfectly sincerely – impressions that are not wholly accurate.'

'No doubt. But the ink was wet.'

'It is not a matter we need pursue farther.' Appleby was studying the housekeeper with a good deal of attention. She was a surprise. She was a surprise not merely because she was herself so decidedly not 'one of the servants' – although it hadn't in fact been mentioned to him that she was a domestic employee of the genteel variety. She was a surprise because she was rather tremendous – a handsome woman in full maturity.

Appleby wondered how long she had been at Urchins. He also wondered what the two recently arrived ladies thought of her. To describe her adequately seemed to call for a rather vulgar Edwardian vocabulary; one would think of phrases like 'charms' and 'ample but alluring proportions.' Yet she wasn't vulgar herself, and she had a presence which quite knocked comedy – let alone farce – out of the picture. Passion smouldered in the black eyes of this intimidating person. If she put on a turn, it would be as a tragedy queen. She could probably scare a man stiff. In fact, one might find oneself allured by her one week, and bolting precipitately from her across Europe the next. Across Europe… Appleby was aware that it wasn't utterly at random that this notion had come into his head. It was just conceivable that here in Mrs Husbands was another factor in the supposedly belated emotional education of Lewis Packford.

'Do I understand,' Mrs Husbands asked, 'that there are other aspects of Mr Packford's death on which you wish to question me?' She spoke very coldly. It was evident that she wouldn't lightly forgive Appleby for occasioning her loss of nerve a few minutes before.

'A short conversation would certainly be very valuable to me.' Appleby glanced at the tray. 'That's a most delicious cold lunch. But perhaps it can wait a little. Shall we sit down?'

Mrs Husbands sat down. 'I see no reason,' she said without cordiality, 'why you shouldn't eat as we talk – if talk we must. It was my impression that the police had satisfied themselves and concluded their inquiries.'

'That would meet with your approval? You feel that nothing more should be done?'

'I feel nothing of the sort. But let the police turn their attention to those women. They should both go to prison.'

'Mrs Packford and the other lady who appears to have – well, some interest in that title? You regard them as implicated in Mr Packford's death?' Appleby, who hadn't adopted the suggestion that he should begin to eat, glanced at Mrs Husbands with what was no more than an air of polite interrogation. But he was now very interested in her indeed. For she had spoken in a sudden flare of anger. If Packford's death had been clamped down, so to speak, under a tolerably firm lid, this was the first really promising jolt it had received.

'Implicated in his death? They caused it.' Mrs Husbands was breathing quickly, but her voice was again under control.

'You mean that they murdered him – the two of them together?'

'Not that. Of course I know that he shot himself. But they drove him to it.'

'I see. Well, that is a very different matter. These ladies may have confronted him with an awkward situation, leading to his committing suicide. But it's not clear that, as a result they should be put in prison.'

'Hadn't they both married him? Isn't that utterly illegal?'

Appleby received this question in thoughtful silence. It was obvious that Mrs Husbands, although only a superior employee, was fully informed of the present situation at Urchins. It was obvious that, although both competent and distinctly frightening, she was not a woman of much intelligence. Either that – or, what was equally tenable at the moment – she was in so deep a state of emotional disturbance over Packford's death that her power of quite ordinary judgement was impaired.

'Illegal?' Appleby said. 'Of course, there has undeniably been illegality somewhere in the business – if, that is to say, two marriages were actually performed and registered. But it is extremely unlikely that the first of the ladies has in any degree broken the law. There would have to be most unusual circumstances of collusion to bring about anything of the sort. And the second lady is much more likely to have been an innocent party than not. I fear, in fact, that your mind is in some confusion in this matter. The only person who had certainly performed a criminal act was Mr Packford himself. But you are disposed to judge him innocent?'

'I judge him base and despicable!'

Appleby received this too in silence for a time. Mrs Husbands, to put it mildly, seemed a little lacking in discretion. For what was emerging from her performance was the portrait of a woman who felt herself to have been betrayed, and who had undergone some violent revulsion of feeling in consequence. It was odd that Cavill had missed so striking an addition to his gallery of psychological types. Not that there was anything out-of-the-way in her. Indeed, in this very house there were two other women upon whom similar emotional confusions might be at play at this very moment. Perhaps Mrs Husbands differed from Ruth chiefly in the disposition to let her hair down in tense situations. As for Alice the barmaid, she was still an unknown quantity.

'It certainly seems,' Appleby said, 'as if the late Mr Packford allowed himself to behave in a manner suggesting some little weakness of character.'

'He was an extremely upright and generous man!' Mrs Husbands had produced this like a flash. She hadn't much power of resistance, Appleby reflected, to the quite elementary wiles which a policeman carries round. About Lewis Packford she would allow herself words as bitter as she could lay her tongue to. But the mildest stricture advanced upon him by anybody else would produce an instantaneous impulse of defence. She was an impulsive woman, and perhaps she was an unstable one. What she didn't seem to be was cunning. But this might be the consequence of her being very cunning indeed. And if she were that, there was every probability that her place wouldn't prove to be entirely in the background of this affair.

'Mr Packford's death,' Appleby said vaguely, 'must have come at the end of a day of great strain for everybody concerned. I

73

understand that both these ladies arrived virtually simultaneously and quite out of the blue.'

'I know nothing about the blue.' Mrs Husbands had managed to achieve again her former cold tone. 'But it was certainly my impression that Mr Packford had received no warning whatever that these predatory persons were about to descend upon him.'

'I see.' Mrs Husband's speech, it occurred to Appleby, was decidedly that of an educated woman. And he wondered how Packford had picked her up. Perhaps she was the widow of someone among his learned and academic acquaintance. 'But is it quite fair to describe them in that way? One of them was his legal wife, after all, and the other believed herself to be so.'

'They are both designing women.'

'Well, let us leave it at that. They both turned up – each announcing herself as Mrs Packford?'

'Precisely that, Sir John. Each had apparently received an anonymous letter, and I suspect that each was acting upon specific advice it had contained. For each arrived with a suitcase, rang the front-door bell, and announced herself as being the – the mistress of the house. I should have said myself that they were mistresses of quite another variety.'

'Again, Mrs Husbands, I don't know that that's quite fair. However, there they were. And this extraordinary situation was presently known to the whole household?'

'Certainly, it was. Our parlour maid came to me, and I went at once to Mr Packford. Naturally, I imagined some insolent imposture. His only suggestion was that I should find these – these ambiguous persons rooms. And then he went in to his friends – Professor Prodger and the rest, who were at tea – and explained.'

'Explained?'

'He explained that he was married. In fact he explained that – rather awkwardly – he was doubly married.'

Mrs Husbands was making a great effort to preserve her cool and acrid tone. 'Canon Rixon has told me that he appeared like a man in a daze.'

'And then?'

'And then the – the two persons dined with Mr Packford and his friends.'

'That must have been extremely queer. Was it your own opinion that Mr Packford was – well, noticeably discomposed?'

'He must have been – if what happened later is to be explained. But it is Canon Rixon's opinion that Mr Packford, although disturbed, didn't really grasp the full gravity of his position. His mind was still largely on something else.'

'On something connected with his work?'

Mrs Husbands nodded. 'Yes – something like that. Some very important discovery which he was proposing to announce to his friends.'

'I find that very interesting.' Appleby – apparently absent-mindedly – had begun to eat his lunch after all. 'In fact, it brings us to something extremely significant, which I should like you to consider very carefully. Have you any reason to believe that this important discovery, which Mr Packford was perhaps about to announce, concerned any physical object that had come into his possession?'

Mrs Husbands looked puzzled. 'I am afraid I don't follow you, Sir John.'

'Well, put it this way. A scholar may arrive at some new and surprising piece of knowledge simply as a matter of inference. He sees a connection, hitherto unappreciated, between facts which are themselves already well known. Or again, research may lead him to some hitherto unexamined book or document in a public collection – say, the library of the British Museum. Or, yet again, he may actually himself acquire a book or a document or a work of art. It may simply be extremely interesting in his particular learned world. Or it may be extremely valuable as well. Have you any opinion as to which of these categories would apply in the matter we are considering?'

'None at all. Mr Packford was never communicative about his discoveries, until he judged that he had found an effective moment for being so. But it is very possible that some of his present guests – of Mr Edward Packford's present guests, I ought to say – may be better informed than I am.'

'Thank you. I wonder if you have anything to add to your account of how you found Mr Packford's body in this room? As I understand the matter, the evening ended early and in considerable restraint?'

'I suppose so. But I hadn't, you will realize, the misfortune to be present. It has never been part of my duties to entertain Mr Packford's guests.'

'Quite so. But I imagine, Mrs Husbands, that you weren't able to avoid being given some account of how things were going?'

'That is certainly true. Both the maids who waited at dinner – I ought to mention, perhaps, that Mr Packford kept no menservants indoors – came to me in some distress, saying that it had been most disagreeable. I told them it was no affair of theirs. And to my own knowledge, of course, the party broke up early. Mr Packford came into this library, as was his invariable custom, for an hour or two before going to bed. And everybody else, it seems, went to their several rooms. But Mr Cavill questioned me very closely about all this.'

'I appreciate that. You went into the drawing-room, I think, about half-past ten, fearing that the servants might have been so occupied with gossip that the coffee and so forth hadn't been cleared away. And it was there you heard the shot?'

'That is corrrect, Sir John.'

'You realized at once that it was, in fact, a revolver shot?'

'No, indeed. My first odd thought was that somebody must be opening a bottle of champagne. And that – very absurdly – took me hurrying towards the dining-room. Then I realized that the sound had certainly come from here, and I hurried in. Mr Packford was dead.'

'Anybody who had been in this room with him at the time of the shot could have got away?'

Mrs Husbands nodded rather wearily. 'Again, Sir John, you are only going over Mr Cavill's ground once more. It is undoubtedly true that anybody could have got away – either into the house, or out through the French window.'

'But, nevertheless, it would only have been a matter of, say, half a minute, either way? There would have been no time for such a person to conduct even a rapid search of this room?'

'I am quite sure there would not.'

Appleby pushed away the tray and stood up. He found he had done full justice to what had been an excellent refection. Indeed, what had been presented to him, together with the implications of some of Mrs Husbands' references to the household over which she presided, prompted Appleby's next line of inquiry. 'Urchins, if I may say so, appears to be run on decidedly liberal lines. Mr Packford was very comfortably off?'

'Certainly. Mr Packford was a small proprietor.'

'Quite so.' Appleby, remembering the lumbering bulk of the dead man, found it hard not to smile at this curious description. It might be called, he supposed, another of the Edwardian touches about Mrs Husbands. 'And you had no reason to suppose that he was in anything that could be called financial embarrassment? There was never any difficulty about the household bills, or matters of that sort?'

'Never.' Mrs Husbands hesitated. 'Beyond that, I have, of course, no knowledge.'

'I suppose not.' Appleby had walked to the desk, and now he tapped the postcard which still lay on it. 'You have heard that this is the beginning of a quotation from Shakespeare – a speech of Cardinal Wolsey's in *Henry VIII*, after his fall? *Farewell, a long farewell, to all my greatness.* You can't think of anything specific that Mr Packford might have thought to refer to in that way? It mightn't refer to an approaching need to live in some much more modest fashion than here at Urchins?'

'I think that very unlikely indeed.' Mrs Husbands spoke with decision. 'It would be much more likely to refer, surely, to his very considerable reputation. I have often been told that Mr Packford was, quite strictly, a great scholar. And he naturally set much more store by that than by the mere fact of being a country gentleman with a small estate. But I don't myself believe that he was thinking either of one sort of greatness or another. He would often produce what were clearly quotations with only a very partial application to the circumstances prompting them.'

'That's something I was aware of in him myself.' Mrs Husbands, it seemed to Appleby, if not very intelligent, was nevertheless a perfectly shrewd woman when unexcited. 'You don't know, I suppose, what happens to Urchins now?'

'Certainly not.'

'I understand from Mr Edward that his late brother's solicitor, a Mr Rood, is coming down this evening about matters of that sort. Do you know him?'

'Yes, I do. He has been here several times. I believe he shared some of Mr Packford's learned interests. Perhaps that is why Mr Packford employed him.'

'You speak, Mrs Husbands, as if you rather distrusted the man.'

'I don't know about that. But I decidedly don't care for him. He appears to me to be simultaneously arid and conceited. It is a combination for which there is nothing to be said.'

'Well, I would agree with the general proposition.' Mrs Husbands, Appleby thought, was certainly possessed of an academic past, and had picked up from it turns of phrase which were not entirely natural to her. She seemed, too, to have a considerable capacity for disapproving of people. And this reflection prompted Appleby to a final, slightly odd question. 'Who would you say,' he asked, 'is the most sensible person about Urchins at the moment?'

Mrs Husbands had picked up the tray and was moving to the door. Her answer came without a moment's hesitation. 'Canon Rixon, without a doubt.'

'Does *he* take a dark view of people?'

'A dark view?' Mrs Husbands almost flushed, so that it was clear that this very mild thrust had gone home. 'Far from it. I should describe him as a benevolent man.'

'I think,' Appleby said, 'I'll have a word with him next. But first I propose to have a further look around this library.'

'To search it, you mean?' Mrs Husbands was very chilly again.

'More or less that.' Appleby crossed the room and politely opened the door. 'And I needn't detain you longer,' he said.

There were, of course, tens of thousands of books – and all, it was clear, of a learned and solid sort. Urchins no doubt ran to a certain amount of light literature. But that would be kept in other apartments, where it could be picked up and laid down again by casual readers without any disturbance of the maturer studies of the owner of the house. Appleby poked about the drawers and cabinets – not with much conviction, since, after all, Cavill had been there before him. He climbed the little spiral staircase and examined some of the very topmost rows of books. These appeared unfrequented, and were not free from a fine film of dust. He guessed that Mrs Husbands had superintended a major cleaning operation of the library during Packford's absence in Italy, and that when he was at home he didn't much like the place to be disturbed. He descended, and studied the manner in which the main collection was arranged on the shelves. There wasn't any very substantial evidence of system. Packford, like many of his kind, probably prided himself on the power of his memory to take him straight to a wanted book. Nevertheless the volumes all had shelf-marks, and there was a substantial card-index in what appeared to be good order. During the immediately preceding few years Packford had taken to noting in this the dates of his acquisitions and purchases. It might be possible, if one had occasion for so laborious a job, to distinguish, by means of this, something of the particular directions in which his mind had been reaching out during the period. But this wasn't an activity which Appleby proposed for himself at the moment.

Nevertheless the books continued to occupy him for some time. Sometimes he stood back, as if to gain some general impression of a substantial section of them. Sometimes he peered minutely at one row or another. He wondered whether Packford had employed an assistant: and, if so, what sort of operations that assistant performed. He might ask Mrs Husbands.

But better not do that, he said to himself as he left the room. It was just possible that he was on to something. If he was, it would be prudent to keep quite, quite dark about it at the moment.

6

Appleby found Canon Rixon in the garden. He was seated in an arbour, playing Snakes and Ladders with a young woman. The Canon was very ugly and the young woman quite ravishingly pretty. She was posed – for it was much as if her companion had deliberately posed her for his own pleasure and Appleby's – in a small shifting dapple of sunlight and shadow. And she was like some commonplace flower in a cottage garden – as such a flower might appear when viewed under the influence of mescalin. Or she might have been something on a canvas of Renoir's. Only that would have been a pity, since then it wouldn't have been possible to take her clothes off.

This last wasn't, perhaps, a proper thought by which to be visited in the presence of a clergyman. But then the Canon himself seemed to take in the young woman a delight which certainly comprehended more than her immortal soul. 'Do you know Alice?' he asked cheerfully when Appleby had introduced himself. 'She ought, you know, to be Alice Packford. Only it seems that she isn't – and that's a great shame. Although, as things have turned out, it wouldn't have made so very much difference – would it, my dear?' He had turned to Alice and – in what, Appleby admitted, was a properly fatherly way – patted the small rosy hand which was holding a dice-box. 'The Archbishop of Canterbury, it is true, might not be in agreement with me. But we must remember that there is to be neither marrying nor giving in marriage later on. So, at least, our recent awkward situation won't simply repeat itself again in heaven. Alice, my child, it's your throw.'

Alice threw vigorously. 'Five!' she cried in triumph. And then her face fell. 'It's the very same horrid snake as last time!'

'So it is.' Rixon shook a commiserating head. 'And you see what a really trying game it is. Compare it with real life. There are any number of snakes in that. But you can't be called upon to visit the tummy of precisely the same snake twice. That is what, in my profession, we call a comfortable thought. Now – let me see.' He rattled the dice-box. 'Four! Dear, dear – it takes me just past the longest ladder on the board.'

'I'll win yet.' Alice rattled with determination. She was clearly dead keen on the game. At the same time she was weeping softly. The tears on her cheeks were like drops of dew on a peach. 'Six! That means I have another turn.'

'Now *there*, you see, Snakes and Ladders *doesn't* differ from life. There's always the possibility of another turn. Not perhaps for an old fellow like myself, but certainly for the young. Six again! That puts you right ahead of me. I'm not sure that this is at all a Christian game. It keeps on upping one person and downing another. Whereas Christianity, as my dear old bishop used to say, puts us all on a common level.'

Appleby watched the game in silence until it ended in Alice's victory. Canon Rixon continued to talk cheerfully throughout, and it had to be concluded that he had his own peculiar system of pastoral care, which he was in fact at present directing upon Alice with some success. Despite the girl's blooming beauty, there was more than her occasional slow tears to show that she had been through deep distress. And unhappiness seemed all wrong for Alice. Appleby could see that any man whose eye rested on her twice might find himself absolutely compelled to do anything in the world to preserve her in a condition of unflawed enjoyment of the world. Perhaps it had been like that with the late Lewis Packford.

And this confirmed itself as soon as Alice began to talk. 'Do you know,' she asked Appleby gravely, 'that nobody has been so nice to me as the Reverend here?' This appeared to be her way of referring to Rixon. 'And that's a thing you'd never expect, now – would you?'

At this Rixon gave Appleby a cheerful wink. 'Alice,' he said, 'you're an ignorant girl. Your knowledge of the beneficed clergy of the Church of England is, I perceive, nebulous. But you're a good child, all the same.'

'And it was true right from the start,' Alice went on. 'I mean, from when I arrived. And I was mad, you know. Oh, my – wasn't I mad!'

Appleby nodded. 'At not being married?'

'Well – that, of course. It was a terrible sell. Yes, it was a terrible let-down. But what I was chiefly mad at was his being so silly. Loo, I mean.'

'Our late friend,' Rixon interpolated.

'I only wanted a ring, you know.' Alice appeared to have embarked upon what she appeared to regard as a process of apology. 'Just a Woolworth ring, like other girls have. There wouldn't – would there? – have been any real harm in that. I mean there wouldn't have been any *more* harm. The Reverend says there wouldn't.'

Rixon coughed. 'In point of fact,' he said to Appleby, 'I believe I used the phrase "*virtually* no more harm." But no matter.'

'And there would have been a nice feeling about it.' Alice paused. 'I must have pestered Loo. It was that bad of me. And one day he simply said we were going to get married – only that we'd keep it quiet. Well, that was all right by me. But I never thought he was doing what he was. Oh, my – I was mad!' She sighed, produced a handkerchief, and wiped away a tear. 'I was in a tearing fury with him that I arrived here. And I think Loo' – suddenly she burst out sobbing – 'got me wrong!'

'Got you wrong?' Appleby considered this. 'You mean your being mad wasn't for the reason he supposed it to be?'

Alice shook her head mutely. She was incapable of reply. And Canon Rixon took it upon himself to explain. 'That is precisely it. Alice felt that her – that Packford had done something extremely dangerous just for her sake. That was it, Alice, wasn't it?'

Alice nodded. 'It's something they put you inside for,' she sobbed. 'I know. They did it to my Uncle Jim. And it wouldn't matter how I lied. Not after it was found out. Because of course it's in writing in the place we were married. They'd be certain to get him. And that's why I was so mad with him – for being so silly just because I'd had a fancy for something. And I think he thought it was because I'd started hating him, the great silly.'

'Yes, I see.' What Appleby was chiefly seeing was Alice's large appeal. Not only were all her tangible and visible surfaces golden. She quite plainly had a heart of gold as well. 'And you're afraid,' he asked, 'that his making that mistake may have – well, got him down?'

'Just that. After all, the others were really hating him.'

'The others?'

'Ruth was really hating him. And the old woman too – his cook. I could see that in her at once.'

'His cook?' Appleby was puzzled.

'Alice means the capable Mrs Husbands,' Rixon interrupted. 'She does, no doubt, supervise the culinary side of the establishment. And she might be described as of full years. I hope Alice exaggerates. It would be quite reasonable that Mrs Husbands should be, shall we say, cross. But hatred is another matter. And as for Ruth, my dear Alice, the fact is that you don't quite understand her type. You haven't come across it, I dare say.'

'You meet all sorts in my trade.' Alice was ingenuously indignant. 'And I'd like you to know that I've always been mostly on the saloon and private-bar side. So I see all the superior ones too, believe me. But it's true that Ruth has me guessing. And what poor Loo could see in a – '

'Quite so, quite so.' Rixon made a restraining gesture. 'But the point, my dear, was this. Ruth was very cold and cutting. But that doesn't mean hate – not in a woman of that type of education, and so forth. Ruth may have been feeling very much as you were. I hope Sir John will bear me out in this.'

Challenged in this way, Appleby felt that there would at least be no harm in a conventional expression of agreement. 'And I don't see,' he added, turning to Alice, 'that you can really have anything with which to reproach yourself. In your attitude, I mean, to Mr Packford just before his death.'

'But, you see, I don't remember!' Alice again applied her handkerchief to her eyes. The fact that she did so with a refined gesture becoming in one on the private-bar side didn't make her woe any less appealing. 'I often don't, when I'm upset. Not since the bottle.'

'Not since the bottle?' Appleby supposed for a moment that this must be an idiom meant to express the period since Alice's first infancy.

'Alice,' Canon Rixon explained, 'was hit on the head with a bottle.' He spoke with the casual ease of a clergyman who prides himself on knowing the world. 'It is, of course, one of the professional risks of the licensed trade.'

'But it was in the snug,' Alice added – as if this circumstance removed the affair somewhat out of the ordinary. 'It was in the snug, and by a very well-conducted gentleman who came in regular as clockwork to listen to the nine o'clock news. He had to be put away, poor soul.'

'And you have been liable,' Appleby asked, 'to bouts of forgetfulness ever since then?'

'Only when I've been upset really bad.' Alice was anxious, it seemed, not to exaggerate this aspect of her personality.

'A purely hysterical amnesia,' Rixon said. There appeared to be few spheres into which his technique of cheerful reassurance didn't reach. 'There is seldom, I understand, anything at all serious in that sort of thing.' He paused. 'Although it must, of course, have its inconveniences.'

'Quite so.' Appleby didn't give much more than civil attention to this. He was looking curiously at the young woman. 'And what happens?' he asked. 'How do you behave when you have these temporary failures of memory?'

'I can't tell, can I?' Alice made this point with a great appearance of reason.

'Well, no.' Appleby smiled as encouragingly as he could, for it struck him that the girl was now rather frightened. 'But I suppose you are given tolerably reliable information about it from time to time?'

'People don't say much. It's kind of awkward, you see.'

'Yes, I do see that.' Appleby was patient. 'And you certainly needn't talk about this at all, if you don't want to.'

Alice took a deep breath. She was helpless before this magnanimity. 'But they do say,' she said, 'that I can behave real queer.'

'And it was like that the other evening? There's a big gap in what you can remember anything about?'

'Yes. From the sweet.'

'From the sweet?' Appleby was puzzled.

Alice blushed. 'What we had at the end. The dessert.'

Rixon chuckled. 'Which the profane vulgar,' he said, 'do denominate pudding.' He patted Alice's hand again. It was something, Appleby reflected, that could quite rapidly build up into a habit.

'Because after that,' Alice went on, 'I can remember nothing at all. Not until I woke up next morning.' She looked at Appleby with large woebegone eyes. 'Not,' she amplified, 'until they woke me up in my own bed with a cup of tea next morning.'

And at this Alice went indoors. Appleby thoughtfully watched her departure. 'I suppose,' he asked Rixon, 'that the poor girl was summoned after the discovery of Packford's death? It wasn't left until that cup of tea?'

'She was certainly summoned. We all were. But I can well believe she was in some state she didn't afterwards remember. There was something somnambulistic about her, without question. She registered what, superficially, one would have called normal shock. And yet there was something odd about it.' Rixon hesitated. 'You don't think, my dear sir, that she could conceivably have been in any way responsible for – '

'One can't, in a business of this sort, afford to rule anything out. And a girl who, on the night of a somewhat mysterious fatality, may have been wandering about in what is called, I believe, a dissociated state certainly mustn't be ignored. Not that I'm so interested in Alice as I am in you.'

'In me?' Canon Rixon was undoubtedly startled by this sudden assault. He had picked up the Snakes and Ladders, and now the dice and counters could be heard to rattle sharply in their box.

'Or in anybody whose connection with the dead man was more on his professional and learned than on his personal and – shall we say? – amorous side. You see, Dr Rixon, the spectacle of a man of Lewis Packford's standing and intelligence being pursued by two enraged wives is so exceedingly surprising that it tends to shove itself into the very centre of the picture. And that may be unjustifiable. It's true that he must have found marriage an extremely interesting experience –'

Rixon nodded. 'The evidence,' he said urbanely, 'points that way.'

'But I doubt whether it was really so absorbing as his work.'

'I rather agree.'

'Well then, consider that scrawled message found on his desk. Accept the straightforward view that Lewis Packford wrote it and then blew his brains out. And accept, too, the supposition that he used that particular quotation not entirely at random. What would be your comment on it?'

'*Farewell, a long farewell, to all my greatness.*' Canon Rixon repeated the words weightily, rather as if they were a text at the start of a sermon. 'Packford's greatness, in Packford's eyes, could mean only his reputation as a scholar – as a person of the most undoubted eminence in his field of literary research. If he felt that he was saying farewell to that, it would be because he had reason to suppose that this reputation was about to suffer some irreparable blow.'

'And just how might that come about?'

'He might have made even more of an ass of himself than we all sometimes do.' Rixon plainly offered this as rather a felicitous formulation. 'Somebody might be in a position to show that one of Packford's major discoveries was moonshine – and in circumstances which would exhibit him as having possessed an embarrassing streak of ignorance, or as having been ludicrously credulous or culpably careless. Nothing of this sounds to me particularly likely, but it is more likely than the other obvious possibility.'

'Which is?'

Rixon hesitated. 'He might not have been frank about his indebtedness to another man's work. That, of course, when sufficiently heinous, means sudden death to a scholar's reputation. Or – yet again – he might have invented evidence to support one or another of his triumphant discoveries. If an exposure of anything of that sort were imminent, then certainly his greatness would be something it was time to say goodbye to.'

Appleby considered this. 'And it is your own opinion, Dr Rixon, that something of the sort was actually blowing up?'

'Decidedly not!' Rixon spoke warmly. 'Quite the contrary. We all had the impression that poor Packford was in a mood of very considerable confidence, that he believed himself to have made a most important new discovery, and that he was on the brink of letting us in on the secret. Sometimes it amused him to let the new cat out of the bag at a simple jump. But more commonly it emerged by inches. There was undoubtedly something of the showman in Packford, and he liked to work up curiosity. It was a trait in him that irritated scholars of the severer and bleaker sort.'

'But he hadn't in fact revealed anything specific? His hints were still vague?'

Rixon took time to consider this question. 'I can't speak for Limbrick,' he said. 'Have you met Limbrick yet?'

'No, I haven't. But he's the next person I must get hold of. I understand that, among other things, he is an important collector? Professor Prodger seems to take a poor view of him.'

'Prodger has become very eccentric, as you must have observed. Limbrick is a wealthy man, who certainly collects manuscripts and rare books and so forth. But he is also something of a scholar in his own right, or he would not be one of our small society.'

'The Bogdown Society?'

Rixon laughed. 'Ah, so you have heard of that? It is only an occasional joke, you know – a mere bagatelle, as they used to say. We are held together, I hope, by more solid interests as well. But what I was saying, Sir John, is this: that Packford may have told Limbrick rather more than the rest of us. That, indeed, is my impression. No doubt you will investigate it.'

'No doubt I shall.' Appleby suddenly looked full at Rixon. 'Did you know that Packford had a vivid interest in the subject of literary forgery?'

'I have heard him talk about it.' Rixon was startled. 'Perhaps he may have projected one of his attractive lighter monographs on the subject.'

'When I called on him in Italy, not very long ago, he made a joke about it. He suggested that he and I should set up as forgers together.'

Rixon laughed – perhaps a shade uneasily. 'That is quite like Packford, is it not? His sense of humour was often freakish, but never subtle.'

'I agree. But in detection, you know – which was my trade until I was nobbled by rather dull administration – one learns always to attend to a man's jokes.'

'Ah!' Rixon nodded competently. 'The Freudian theory of wit, eh? Very interesting. Very interesting indeed.'

'Perhaps you can call it that. It's perhaps true that a joke often represents the bringing out for an airing of something slightly disreputable or risky. The joke-element is a sort of disguise.'

Canon Rixon weighed this for a moment, and then seemed to decide that it called for a distinct change of tone. 'I don't like anything of this,' he said. 'It is trafficking in suspicions in a fashion that is extremely repugnant to me. And I don't believe that Lewis Packford had the slightest inclination to perpetrate literary forgeries. I blame myself for having entered into the subject.'

'You would be quite wrong if you refused to do so.' Appleby had now stood up, and he spoke energetically. 'It seems to me that Packford's death still preserves a grave element of unresolved doubt. You would act very improperly if you were not as fully communicative as it is possible to be.'

'That is perfectly true.' Rixon, too, rose. 'But I don't believe that poor Packford had a hankering after forgery, all the same.'

Appleby shook his head a shade impatiently. 'My dear sir, I am not myself asserting anything of the sort. It may have been something quite different that prompted him to discuss the subject with me. I see at least two further possibilities.' Appleby paused. 'And one of them strikes me as really interesting.'

7

The trouble about this nebulous affair – Appleby told himself as he took a turn round the garden – consists in its being so full of implausible possibilities. Make the one assumption that Mrs Husbands is for some reason unreliable about the ink on that postcard, and all sorts of queer notions are in order.

Take, for instance, Mrs Husbands herself. It's perfectly clear that she had strong feelings about her employer. One can't, indeed, speak confidently of an emotional relationship between them. That may have existed; but, even if it did, it can't at present be identified. On the other hand, the intensity of feeling may have been all on the lady's side, and Lewis Packford scarcely aware of it. Mrs Husbands is the younger by a good many years, but she may nevertheless have built up for herself a maternal rather than an amorous role. It's clear that she was instantly prompted to an overwhelming jealousy of the two young women who had so strangely turned up with intimate claims upon Packford. That fits in reasonably enough with either interpretation of the nature of her feelings. But when you come to the hypothesis of murder – of a full-blown *crime passionnel* – it's quite a different matter. Women don't possess themselves of army revolvers and shoot their dream sons. But they do occasionally behave in that way with their dream lovers.

Then take the two other ladies. Ruth Packford represents another implausible possibility. She is a wronged wife. She is – Appleby insisted to himself – a rather badly wronged wife: and what was variously engaging in Packford's character mustn't blind one to that.

91

The man behaved in a weak and shabby fashion. And then, quite suddenly and ignominiously, he was exposed. In such a situation plenty of women have got to work with revolvers – and, for that matter, with knives and hatchets and packets of rat-poison – before now. So the implausibility here may be superficial and delusory, and proceed chiefly from the lady's professed attitude and from her degree of education. Yes, particularly, perhaps, from this last. When, hard upon her husband's death, a lady takes to lecturing you on the latest contribution to our knowledge of Thomas Horscroft to have been achieved by an American professor, one instinctively writes her off as a very high-powered emotional dynamo. But this, conceivably, is rash. It is often, after all, inhibited and highly cerebral types that surprisingly fly off the handle.

And then – Appleby said to himself – there's Alice. Alice's morals are no doubt to be regretted, but there is every sign that she rose to her crisis like an angel. About Ruth's fair-mindedness and objectivity one can feel doubts. Even if she is entirely innocent of her husband's death, there is still a sense of strain – even of something factitious – about her manner. But Alice, no one with any experience of human nature would think of twice in connection with such an affair as the present. She has plainly never hurt a fly. But then about Alice there is a fantastic and imponderable factor. She was hit on the head with that bottle.

One can't make much of that. It's a matter for medical experts, and almost certainly one will say one thing and another will flatly contradict him. So far, that is to say, as the theoretical possibilities go. Alice, of course, may have a history. She knows that she behaves queerly when she has an attack; and if that queerness turns out to include a disposition to major acts of violence – well, that will be too bad for her. And it isn't, I suppose, an impossibility. One is told that it is the people with hearts of gold who find themselves living beyond their moral income and liable to catastrophic irruptions from submerged areas of their personality. Still, I'm damned if it isn't the most implausible notion of the lot. Not that I'm inclined to write off Alice's amnesia altogether. Even if it didn't take her into that library with a gun – and where on earth, poor child, would she get a gun from? – it may prove to be not without its significant impact on the case.

So much for the women, Appleby said to himself – and paused to look around him. The gardens on this side of the house were in excellent order, but this only made Urchins itself more obviously in need of repair. There were spots in which things were going badly wrong with the fabric – and largely through a neglect of quite simple attention to pointing and painting. Lewis Packford had been full of a large vague enthusiasm for the little villa he had taken on Lake Garda for a season, but he didn't seem much to have bothered about this substantial property which had come down to him from his fathers. Which brings me – Appleby thought – to Edward.

What about fratricide? It is, after all, among the things that happen from time to time. Usually it is true, among the feeble-minded or the criminal sections of the community. But it mustn't be ruled out simply because the present affair has, with the pleasing exception of Alice, a pervasively upper-class dramatis personae. It's more relevant to consider that Edward claims to have been in Paris when his brother died. But I don't suppose that Cavill, in the circumstances, felt it necessary to do much in the way of testing out that alibi. So suppose that Edward really came back that evening, went straight and unobserved to his brother in the library, and there learnt that Urchins was now graced by two ladies claiming to be Mrs Packford. Can one endow Edward with the sort of temperament for which this was, so to speak, a last straw? Imagine him as deeply devoted to Urchins – there is, after all, something about his own room here that denotes a nostalgic type of mind – and as for long mountingly indignant at Lewis' neglect of it. And then suppose him suddenly confronted with this culminating mess…

Appleby shook his head. It's unbelievable, he told himself. Taken just like that, it's unbelievable. It's true there's something about Edward, something I can't precisely focus, that makes me feel an odd lingering doubt about him. And Edward said something that stuck in my head; he said he believed he'd be rather good at executing summary justice. But it's still implausible. One doesn't kill a brother because he's improvident, or careless in little matters of estate management. And not even – except in some ancient romances – for doing something disgraceful, and dishonouring the family name. Only the suffering of some deep personal wrong would begin to make sense of Edward Packford as a suspect. I can't say that such a wrong wasn't suffered. But at least I haven't the slightest evidence of its existence.

Appleby brought out a pipe and filled it. He would allow himself any inspiration it might bring, before he returned to the house and made some further contacts. He must see his host again, and put himself in the way of accepting an invitation for the night. Because now he wanted that. He wanted to be about when his old acquaintance Mr Rood appeared bearing Lewis Packford's will. And he also wanted to be about later – perhaps much later – than that. And here – he said to himself, with his pipe going well – I come to the real nub to the matter. All this business of wives, and of everything in the way of disturbed personal relations which may flow from them, is a monstrous red herring. It's just like Lewis Packford to have made his farewells to this life with a large bad distracting joke in the worst of taste. One is sorry for Ruth and Alice. They have been extremely badly treated; their position is humiliating and absurd; and of course, according to their degree of affection for the dead man, it is sad, tragic, or what you will. *But they have nothing to do with the case.*

Appleby sat down on a garden bench – almost as if to give himself an opportunity of staring stoutly at this bold proposition. The entire mystery, if mystery there was, lay, so to speak, on the other frontier of Lewis Packford's life. The suspicions of Professor Prodger were crack-brained. The suspicions of Mr Rood had appeared, on first impact, to be hardly less extravagant. Men just don't get killed – very seldom, even, kill themselves – in a context of learned discoveries about Shakespeare's Italian travels. Whereas, of course, wives – whether singly or in plurality – are quite another matter. In one way or another, wives have been mixed up with crimes of violence since the beginning of time.

Notwithstanding which – Appleby told himself obstinately as he puffed at his pipe – the true scent in this business began with Lewis Packford spouting out of *Romeo and Juliet*, and being cagey about Verona, and expatiating on the history of literary forgery. It continued through Rood's persuasion that his death was connected with the theft of the physical vehicle of some important discovery in the Shakespearian field. And it culminated – for the moment – in something rather odd that Appleby believed himself to have noticed about Packford's library. There was a possibility, indeed, that one or another or all of the ladies who at present adorned Urchins had some functional role in the mystery. But the mystery was a mystery stemming from the impoverished nobleman of Verona. Appleby wasn't convinced that the impoverished nobleman existed. But he was important, were he fact or fiction.

Appleby got to his feet again and moved on. All this was excellent. It represented the detective intelligence taking a strong and confident line. Unfortunately it was no more than a sort of hunch, and it might be blown to the four winds tomorrow. And decidedly there were some awkwardly missing bits. The poet Meredith had observed, very truly, that in tragic life, God wot, no villain need be. But it wasn't a proposition that held in the present case. If Cavill wasn't right, after all, if the whole affair wasn't what Packford himself had liked to call cobweb, then a villain must be laid on. So far, there hadn't been a glimpse of him. If Rood had anyone in his head, he had bolted from that taxi before giving a name to him. Professor Prodger would scarcely make a convincing villain even in a *milieu* of low comedy in the Anglo-Irish theatre. Canon Rixon, it was true, was ugly enough to play First Murderer in *The Babes in the Wood* – but it was hard to believe that he would not be better accommodated with the part of the Good Fairy.

At this point in his reflection Appleby turned the corner of a tall cypress hedge and came upon a scene of subdued drama.

'How dare you make such a suggestion to me!'

It was very much as if to the missing villain of the piece that Ruth Packford was thus delivering herself. She had, apparently, just sprung to her feet from a chair set beside a low rustic table. On the other side of this, and making no effort to rise to his feet in turn, was a middle-aged man whom Appleby – most unprofessionally – took a strong dislike to on sight. He was very well preserved, and very well dressed, and he now wore an expression of contemptuous surprise. If Ruth's words had been 'Unhand me, sir!' they would have been emotionally correct but factually unwarranted. For the man's hands were occupied already. One of them held a fountain-pen, and the other an object which it took Appleby only a further second to identify as a cheque-book.

This was mildly perplexing, and for a moment Appleby could think of no better explanation than that the well-dressed person had been advancing the most grossly improper of proposals. In which case, no doubt, it was Appleby's business, in the absence of the actual *jeune premier* of the piece, to step forward and incontinently knock him down. Ruth however didn't seem to judge this a necessary move. For she at once put on a bright but icy social manner. 'Sir John,' she said, 'may I introduce Mr Limbrick? Sir John Appleby.'

'How do you do.' Limbrick now rose gracefully and shook hands. 'Mrs Packford and I have been considering some business matters. But they can be deferred. Indeed, perhaps they had better be deferred.' He smiled charmingly. 'Another time, dear lady.'

Ruth could be seen positively to quiver with indignation under this mode of address. 'Thank you,' she said. 'But there will certainly be no occasion to raise the matter again, so far as I am concerned. I have no reason to doubt that my husband had some reasonable occasion to value your society. But I confess it is not apparent to me.' Ruth's icy manner carried her thus far very successfully. But then it turned to a flash of anger. 'Nor, sir, am I accustomed to the society of hucksters. Good afternoon!' And she swung round and marched off.

Limbrick looked at Appleby, slightly shrugged his shoulders, and sat down again. 'Too bad,' he said. 'I only wanted the books.'

Appleby sat down too. He continued to have small fancy for his new acquaintance. But it was his business to continue his inquiries in as amiable a fashion as might be. 'You were proposing,' he asked, 'to buy Lewis Packford's books?'

'Just that.' Entirely without embarrassment, Limbrick put the cheque-book away in his pocket.

'The whole lot? It's a very large library, surely – and is it certain to be Mrs Packford's?'

'Oh, yes – if she is Mrs Packford. And I explained that my offer was conditional upon that. Perhaps I made a mistake there. Perhaps it wasn't entirely tactful. But I don't think I'm likely to be wrong about the legal position. The books are without doubt our late friend's private property. And as the house and estate probably have to go to the brother, it's all the more certain that the rest will go to his wife. Except, of course, what he may have taken it into his head to leave to the little tart from the pub. And that would hardly be sixteenth-century books.'

'I suppose not.' Appleby, who didn't much care for this manner of speaking of Alice, looked at Limbrick stonily. 'But there does seem something rather precipitate in your proposal, all the same. Packford is barely buried. The contents of his will have not yet been communicated to the persons interested. And a library of that sort can't, surely, be bought and sold by the yard? How on earth could you know, even approximately, what would be a fair offer for it?'

Limbrick laughed carelessly. 'I was prepared to go pretty high.'

'I see. And the idea was a binding deal here and now?'

'Just that, Sir John.' Limbrick's tone was faintly mocking. 'One gets nowhere as a collector nowadays if one doesn't act with speed. Too many Americans in the market. Confound them for a set of purse-proud devils!'

Appleby didn't, for a moment, find anything to reply to this. A man prepared to go pretty high in the matter of buying a large library the value of which could only be approximately known to him, and setting about the business by literally thrusting a cheque-book beneath the nose of a woman not a week widowed, seemed to have little title to asperse purse-proud devils, whether on one side of the Atlantic or the other.

And Limbrick was – even in Appleby's fairly extensive experience of men and manners – something new. Wealthy and fanatical collectors, actuated by mere acquisitiveness, are frequently found with a mania for jewels, and sometimes with a mania for pictures. But Appleby had never before met any who went after books and manuscripts in quite what appeared to be Limbrick's spirit. He had indeed heard of their existence, and in the present state of affairs at Urchins he found the actual appearance of such a person a circumstance to ponder on. He also reflected that Professor Prodger was perhaps after all not without discrimination – even although he seemed inclined to confound under one judgement the surely harmless Canon Rixon and this far from agreeable customer. 'You would like Packford's whole collection?' he asked civilly. 'It isn't just a matter of certain very important and interesting items, such as you could go after if the executors held a sale?'

For the first time, Limbrick favoured Appleby with a glance which might have been called closely considering. 'It seems to me,' he said, 'that you may imagine that I've been trying to put over a fast one. That sort of thing is, I suppose, your job. But don't waste your time. Even if that girl had signed on the dotted line, here and now on this table, there would have had to be a valuation for probate, and so on. I couldn't really have got away with anything.' Limbrick smiled insolently. 'Or not, at least, with very much.'

'If we discuss that sort of thing, Mr Limbrick, perhaps you'll bear in mind that it was you who raised it, and not me. But there is one question I'd be curious to hear your answer to. Were you having a shot at securing only such books as are in this house at this moment, or were you proposing to buy any other book, in any other place, which may be legally part of the estate of the dead man?'

'The second, naturally. With a collection like Packford's, you see, there are always likely to be volumes away on loan, and other volumes away at the binder's. So when one does buy an entire library – and it's not so uncommon a proceeding as you appear to think, my dear sir –

one takes care that such contingencies are allowed for. I think, by the way, that you may have rather an exaggerated idea about the value of books – of the sort of books, I mean, that are collected by a fellow like Packford.'

'It is, at least, a very large collection.'

'That's perfectly true. There was a big library here before our late friend got going at all. It's not particularly interesting or valuable. But I don't myself despise it. In fact, I want it – as I've explained to you.' Limbrick was now speaking with a great air of candour. 'I'm quite a new man, you see, so far as this sort of thing is concerned. And what I possess, in the way of books, is a small and very tolerably choice collection. What is here at Urchins is, in the main, an extensive and representative sort of library, built up by a good many generations of cultivated people. And that's something I'll be glad to have. But now let me return to Lewis Packford's own additions to it. What he has added is essentially the working library of a scholar. It's fairly valuable, since he spent quite a lot of money, both knowledgeably and on a constantly rising market, over a long period of years. But don't imagine that it contains anything fabulous. It doesn't.'

'I see.' Appleby's tone was that of one who is receiving instruction. 'It certainly wouldn't contain, say, the most valuable book in the world?'

Limbrick began to laugh – and then swung round as his laughter was echoed on a shriller note behind him. Professor Prodger had appeared round the hedge. He peered first at Appleby and then – without any particular appearance of malevolence – at Limbrick. 'A most interesting topic for discussion,' he said. 'The most valuable book in the world. Most interesting. But let us define our terms. Let us not propose to go back beyond the cradle of printing. *Incunabula*, yes. But manuscripts, codices, scrolls, papyri and the like, no. They are not our present concern, not our present concern at all.' Professor Prodger sat down comfortably before the rustic table, and disposed the lower fringe of his beard over its surface. He seemed to feel that the afternoon was before them. 'We can say one thing about the hypothetical subject of our discussion,' he went on. 'It is something that you, Limbrick, would like to possess. Eh?'

'That depends.' Limbrick appeared to find Prodger's arrival disconcerting, and he spoke cautiously.

'No, it doesn't, my dear fellow. It precisely doesn't. *What* the book was – apart from its being the most valuable book in the world – wouldn't matter at all. What you would like to possess, you know, would be simply the particular object in this particular category of objects – to wit, printed books – that the other fellow would be prepared to give most money for. The other person being that fellow Sankey, or somebody like that.'

'Sankey? I've never heard of him.'

'In Chicago, I believe. A meat-king, no doubt. But there are half a dozen others, I believe.' Prodger turned to Appleby. 'And Limbrick,' he added with satisfaction, 'is very small beer, compared with any of them. If the most valuable book in the world ever comes into the open market, it won't be Limbrick who adds it to his collection.' Prodger gave his guinea-pig's laugh. 'But what is it likely to be?' He turned to Appleby. 'Have you any opinion on the matter, Doctor?'

Appleby shook his head. 'I don't know that I have. Not, that is to say, if it's a matter of a printed book. I'd have thought something unique would be more valuable – although no doubt there are printed books of which only one copy is extant. But what about a diary, or something similar? A diary of Shakespeare's, say, with jottings of his ideas for plays. Or his travel-diary. What about something like that?'

For a moment this question met only silence, and Appleby wondered if he was right in instantly feeling something new and wary in the air. 'Most interesting,' Limbrick said presently. 'And perhaps it was something that our late friend said that has put such a notion in your head? Poor Packford would have loved to discover something like that. Prodger, you agree?'

'Certainly, certainly. And Packford *had*, you know, discovered something. And I wouldn't positively say that he hadn't hinted to me' – and Prodger contrived to look extremely cunning – 'that Italy somehow came into it. Limbrick, had you by any chance the same impression?'

Limbrick appeared to be undecided whether he wanted to give an answer to this or not. 'Packford's talk was often misleading,' he said.

'No doubt, no doubt. And we are straying from our topic. A diary or commonplace-book won't do. Our book must be in print. But, even so, its value may reside in something else. The possibility of marginalia suggests itself. For example, a printed book, every available margin of which has been scribbled over by Coleridge, is likely to be of very considerable value. Were the scribbler Milton, the value would be greater still. And were Shakespeare in question' – Prodger's appearance of vast cunning increased – 'we should be, to use a commercial expression, right at the top of the market. Right at the very top, eh? And I couldn't be absolutely certain that Packford wasn't a little disposed to hint at something like that. Not your flight, my dear Limbrick. Not your flight at all. Sankey would be the man for something of that sort.'

Appleby had listened in silence to this obscure sparring. But now he decided on a little exploration. 'Packford's solicitor,' he said, 'has made a similar suggestion to me. Packford, he believes, had come into possession of something very valuable – and of just the sort we have been considering. But Packford was being very close about it. Following an old habit of his, he was beginning to drop a few hints – but nothing really specific. I wonder whether you would both agree that, just before his death, there was a general sense among you that something of the sort was in the wind?'

Prodger nodded his head, so that his beard slithered to and fro on the table. 'Certainly,' he said. 'There can't be a doubt about it. Limbrick, you would support me in that?'

'Yes, I would. But, of course, Packford may have been a little less vague with some of us than with others.'

Appleby thought for a moment. 'The crucial point,' he said, 'appears to me to be this. The valuable object, if of the nature we have been considering, was not intrinsically and self-evidently valuable. An old commonplace-book or still more an old printed book with some writing in it, might have been acquired by Packford from somebody quite uninterested and unlikely ever to give another thought to the matter. And as long as Packford remained secretive about it, he was really in a position of some danger, simply as a consequence of that. Do I make myself clear?'

Limbrick gave an easy laugh. 'Of course you do. A criminal with the necessary specialized knowledge could murder Packford, steal this valuable object, and then simply turn up with it later as his own lawful property, having invented some plausible yarn as to how it came into his possession. There would be no one to challenge him about the thing. You mentioned Packford's solicitor. Is that how his mind is working?'

'I believe it is. But you can ask him tonight. I understand that he is coming down to Urchins with Packford's will.'

Prodger's beard rustled again. 'It occurs to me,' he said, 'that Packford, although he has spoken only in the vaguest terms of this supposed find, may have mentioned it specifically in his will. Or if not there, yet in some paper that is bound to turn up as a consequence of his death. So Limbrick's criminal – in whose existence I am perfectly willing to believe, collectors being what they so notoriously are – must still be going through rather an anxious time. He cannot yet be sure that the precise nature of the pilfered object will not, in fact, be revealed through some such instrumentality as I have indicated. If it is, his crime will have been in vain, since the object will thereby cease to be safely negotiable.'

'Even,' Limbrick asked, 'with collectors being what they so notoriously are? He could still get some sort of price, perhaps, on a clandestine basis. I doubt whether Sir John is entirely neglecting that.'

Appleby nodded. 'You are quite right. The most valuable book in the world would no doubt command a price even if it were drenched in blood. A murderer could, if he knew his market, get money for it readily enough. But so could a much less desperate fugitive from justice. Clearly one has to consider *that*.'

8

The autumn afternoon would soon be over, but Appleby continued his prowl round Urchins. He had decided to spend the night there if Edward Packford invited him. But he rather thought he would make off to the nearest pub for dinner, thereby relieving the household for a time of what was, after all, a somewhat awkward professional presence. Meanwhile he would complete his circuit of the building.

It was thus that he came upon a stable-yard. Like many places of its kind, this now smelt not of horses but of oil and petrol. Along one side a row of loose boxes had been adapted to accommodate half-a-dozen cars, and there were in fact five standing side by side now. One was the ancient affair with which Ruth had met Appleby that morning, and some of the others presumably belonged either to Edward Packford or to the guests whom he had so amiably taken over from his dead brother. But presumably one must have been the property of Lewis Packford himself. Appleby was wondering which it might be – although the speculation didn't seem very material – when the old gardener whom he had seen at the time of his arrival went past wheeling a barrow. Appleby spoke to him. 'Good evening,' he said. 'Now, which would have been Mr Packford's car, and which Mr Edward's?'

'Mr Packford's car?' The old man shook his head. 'We called 'un Mr Lewis here – them that had worked here man and boy as I han.'

'Ah, yes – no doubt you knew his father. And which is his car?'

The old man again shook his head – this time with a more pronouncedly negative suggestion. 'Mr Packford never did have a car, sir. He was always one for fine horses, like.'

'I see. But I mean Mr Lewis. Which is his car, and which is his brother's?'

For a moment the old man appeared to be regarding all this curiosity as uncivil. But then he extended a gnarled hand. 'That be Mr Edward's, sir – the green 'un with the dust still on it. Mr Edward, 'e did have 'un out this morning, and that young varmint Tom bain't got round to it. But Mr Lewis', sir, that be the big 'un with the good shine to it. It hasn't been touched since the death, sir. Mr Edward's special orders.'

'Thank you.' Appleby nodded and strolled away. But when the old man had departed he retraced his steps. Lewis Packford's car was a large, undistinguished and fairly new saloon. Appleby went up and peered into it. He tried the doors and found that they were unlocked. He tried the boot, and found that this was unlocked too. He opened it and discovered that it contained a suitcase. He felt the weight of this. It certainly wasn't empty. He shifted it to try the lid. The catches slid back. He had raised the lid and was peering inside when a voice spoke ironically behind him.

'I suppose it's your feeling that there will be a sale? Mr Limbrick will get the books, and you will get the old clothes. So you're poking round: Is that the idea?'

'I wouldn't call these *old* clothes.' Appleby turned and confronted Ruth. She had put on an overcoat, and had the air of one who is prepared for an expedition. 'It's true they're not new, but I wouldn't call them shabby. And, even when they're neatly folded like this, it's possible to guess they came from a decent tailor. Have a look at them, will you?'

Ruth came up and looked. 'Well?' she asked challengingly.

'It's not quite clear to me, you know, just how much domestic life you and your husband managed together. Would it run to your being able to identify his clothes? In fact, are these his?'

Ruth took another look. 'Yes,' she said firmly. 'They are certainly Lewis'. And so is the suitcase.'

'And do you recognize the packing, as well as the things packed?'

She turned and stared at him. 'I don't understand you.'

'It's quite simple. Is that how Lewis Packford packed?'

'Pecks of pickled pepper.' Ruth offered this facetious response rather desperately. Then she shook her head. 'No – it isn't. And it isn't how I pack, either.'

'That is an additional point of interest, no doubt.' Appleby poked at the topmost garments. 'He didn't keep a manservant. But perhaps Mrs Husbands, or a housemaid, packed for him. Would you say it's like that sort of packing?'

'Not quite.' Ruth now spoke slowly. 'It's certainly not by Lewis, I'm sure. He would chuck things in anyhow. On the other hand, it doesn't strike me as being by what you would call a professional. Not, you know, that I live in a world of valets and lady's maids – as you, Sir John, no doubt do. So my opinion is not authoritative. It's a careful job, but an amateur one. That's my opinion – for what it's worth.'

'I should always value your opinion.' Appleby said this with a courtesy that didn't sound wholly ironic. 'There's a smaller case here as well. Shall we open it too?' He lifted up a square leather case, not much bigger than a handbag.

'We?' Ruth looked at Appleby with some indignation. 'I don't know that I've taken on the post of your first assistant. But open away. It's clear enough what it is: a useless little collection of brushes and bottles and things of the kind that some women travel with.'

Appleby opened the case and confirmed this prediction. 'I suppose you're not,' he asked coolly, 'dissimulating the fact that it's your property?'

'Certainly not. I don't traipse around with an affair of that sort.'

'I don't think Alice would be so scornful of it. In fact, at a guess, I'd say it was hers, and that she's rather proud of it.' Quite casually, Appleby shut down first the little travelling case and then the boot of the car. 'So what does our discovery suggest?'

'I'd rather not talk about it.' Ruth's voice was steady, but her lip was slightly trembling. 'And now I'd better go about my business. I've promised Edward to go and fetch this man Rood. I suppose you wouldn't like the run?'

Appleby was surprised. He was even – rather absurdly – pleased. 'I'll certainly come,' he said. 'But I'll go in and see Edward first. It's my notion to get a meal elsewhere, and then come back to Urchins for the night.'

Ruth nodded. 'I don't grudge you a quiet grill and a pint of bitter. The Husbands cuisine is rather distinguished. But I'm bound to confess I'm getting a bit tired of the conditions under which I'm privileged to partake of it.'

Appleby laughed. 'I have a feeling,' he said, 'that Edward Packford's protracted house-party will soon be breaking up.'

They found Mr Rood at a point outside the railway station at which he could scan the road from Urchins. He had, it appeared, made one of his Napoleonic changes of plan, caught a motor coach, and thus contrived to arrive early. But as he had twin suitcases each rather heavier than there seemed any occasion for, and had therefore been indisposed to wander round seeking a further conveyance, his strategy hadn't resulted in any particular advantage. Except that he had exchanged his silk hat for a bowler, he presented precisely the appearance under which Appleby had first encountered him. And his manner too was unchanged. Having apparently been apprised of the peculiar marital status of his deceased client, he took early occasion to deliver himself to Ruth of sundry conventional sentiments on the theme of sad occasions, distressing circumstances, and the like. These Ruth received with patience. 'You know Sir John Appleby?' she said.

'Certainly I do.' Rood limply shook hands. 'And I was very glad to see he had taken the matter up. Although I disapprove, of course, the deplorably sensational cast of the report.'

'What's that?' Appleby was startled.

Rood was already climbing into the back of the old car. But now he paused to rummage in the pocket of his overcoat. 'Perhaps,' he said, 'you haven't yet seen the evening paper. Allow me.'

Appleby took the newspaper and got in beside Ruth. The death of Lewis Packford, he found, had belatedly made the front page. So had something vaguely described as 'a priceless Shakespeare relic'. The police, the report declared, now thought it highly probable that Packford had died as the result of foul play, and that the priceless relic had been stolen at the same time. There was also a photograph of Appleby – which was something that Appleby always particularly disliked seeing.

Ruth had read the report over his shoulder. She now started up the car. 'At least,' she said, 'there's nothing about bigamy – yet.'

'That is certainly something,' Rood said from the back. 'But one wouldn't expect anything of the sort, until they felt very sure of their ground. They have of course no consideration for the personal feelings of those involved in this deplorable affair. But at least they keep an eye on the law of libel. If they announced that my late client had conspired with – um – the young person now at Urchins to commit bigamy, and the allegation turned out to be without substance, we should have them. We should have them very nicely. Unfortunately, when this further trouble does emerge into daylight, there will be very little we can do. From the point of view of my late client's reputation, the whole affair is truly lamentable. And, of course, for others concerned as well.'

Appleby tapped the evening paper. 'But doesn't this represent pretty well your own view of the case? Isn't this Shakespeare relic they talk about simply a journalist's term for what you suppose Packford to have got from that impoverished nobleman of Verona? And don't you believe that he was, in fact, murdered? Or has the discovery that he'd got into that desperate scrape over marriage now persuaded you to take another view?'

Rood took time to consider this battery of questions carefully. 'I must still incline,' he said presently, 'to my former opinion. I was shown, you know, that postcard purporting to be poor Packford's last message. And I was convinced it is a forgery.'

'If so, Mr Rood, it is certainly an uncommonly good one. Our experts accept it as genuine, and although I understand you have some knowledge of these matters yourself, you are at least outvoted on the point, so far.'

'It's certainly an uncommonly good forgery. It might be called a brilliant forgery. That, my dear sir, is simply part of my case.'

Ruth had begun to drive fast through the dusk, so that the Thomas Horscroft country was slipping by in rather an alarming fashion. But now she slackened pace and spoke. 'I know nothing about this point technically,' she said. 'But I see no reason to suppose that Lewis didn't write that message. There's sense in it. Just what sense, Sir John and I discovered less than an hour ago. It's perfectly plain that Lewis and Alice had decided to cut and run for it. In fact, the long farewell was to me.'

'I am extremely sorry that you should have occasion to suppose so.' Rood got a maximum of unfeeling quality into this, combined with a large suggestion of gloom. 'At the same time, I am not without a suspicion that you may be introducing an unwarranted simplification into your view of the matter. That your husband had decided to cut and run for it is conceivable. Indeed, I am sorry to say that I am myself the bearer of information which enhances the credibility of such a supposition.' Rood had fallen to his favourite occupation of rolling his umbrella. 'But it must nevertheless be evident, my dear madam, that such an intention – and even the taking of certain definite steps to put it into execution – is not incompatible with the sadly sinister interpretation of our melancholy occasion to which I myself find it necessary to incline.'

A speech so heavy as this was not unnaturally followed by an interval of silence. Urchins Pydell went dimly by. And then Ruth spoke abruptly. 'Just what did you mean by that about being a bearer of information making it the more likely that Lewis was thinking of bolting?'

'There is no reason for reticence in the matter. You must certainly know at once, and so must the dead man's brother. Sir John's discretion is doubtless impeccable.' Rood paused as if for a word of thanks for this testimonial. Not getting it, he pursued his ponderous course. 'I have made a careful preliminary investigation of Lewis Packford's affairs. I ought to say at once that I have not myself hitherto had much concern with them on their financial side. Had they been substantially in my hands, I should conceive myself to be gravely indicted of irresponsibility by the deplorable posture in which they now stand.'

'Is all this,' Ruth asked, 'a way of saying that Lewis had been living beyond his means?'

'Certainly that. He appears to have been entirely careless. I fear that there are grave difficulties confronting his estate.'

'But you don't suggest,' Appleby asked, 'that there was anything discreditable behind his difficulties? Apart from his recent queer aberration in contracting two marriages – which is quite another matter – there was nothing more culpable than a rather large inability to bother himself with his own practical affairs?'

'That is, I think, true.' Rood could be glimpsed in the driving-mirror as nodding gravely. 'There were, so far as I know, no – um – irregular courses.'

'You mean women – *more* women?' Ruth asked this challengingly. 'What about Italy?' She turned to Appleby. 'You visited Lewis there, it seems. Were there any signs there of what Mr Rood calls irregular courses?'

Appleby smiled. 'I can't say that there were. He flirted with his cook, but she was in her seventies. He talked about amorous shrimps. But they turned out to be wall paintings.'

'Exactly,' Rood said. 'One is happy to think that there was no vice in him – or not of any positively degrading sort.'

'You put it very nicely.' Ruth spoke in a more acrid tone than Appleby had heard her use before. 'Alice would be grateful to you, too.'

'Would you say that Packford was in any sense a gambler?' Appleby asked this chiefly by way of gliding over an awkward moment. 'A man can quickly lose a great deal, that way.'

'And he can quickly gain a great deal, too.' Rood made this reply rather surprisingly. 'To my mind, there is something we are bound a little to admire in the true gambler's temper. To win handsomely, and then double one's stake, must at least take resolution. But the answer to your question is quite simple. Packford didn't gamble. He didn't even, in the substantial sense, speculate. Had he done so, he might well have come to grief long before now. For, able though he was, there was something guileless and even credulous about him. Not, perhaps, as a scholar. But certainly in life's larger relations. He could, in the vulgar but useful phrase, be had.'

There was another pause, in which Appleby could feel Ruth punch the accelerator. She wasn't at all slow, it occurred to him, to take Rood's pontificatings in a personal sense. 'You'll drop me at that pub?' he asked. 'I'll get back to Urchins about nine.'

Ruth nodded. 'Very well. And I hope you'll have done something about it.'

'Something about it?'

'You arrived this morning and announced that there was a mystery about Lewis' death, after all. I hope you'll arrive again tonight announcing that you've brought the solution.'

'Hardly that.' Appleby spoke seriously. 'But I might well bring a part of it.'

9

The hotel before which Appleby found himself deposited was called 'The Crossed Hands' – so that he wondered whether Thomas Horscroft had found in it an irony sufficiently pungent to be commented on by the Princeton professor. It hadn't been reconstructed lately, and therefore it didn't look particularly antique, but there was a certain undisturbed solidity about it which seemed to promise a decent meal. The lounge was quiet and shabby, with large Victorian steel engravings depicting various more or less catastrophic occasions in English history: the execution of Mary Queen of Scots at Fotheringhay Castle, the trial of Charles the First, the death of General Gordon. There was even Thomas Chatterton clutching a phial of poison in his garret, so that Appleby was appropriately able to reflect on his obscurely significant conversation with Lewis Packford at Lake Garda.

But was it so obscure? He sat down and ordered himself a drink. Wasn't there, indeed – as he had rather rashly hinted to Ruth – a first glimmer of light beginning to break on the whole affair? He had at least arrived at one substantial certainty; and he looked back with some amusement to the moment to which he was indebted for it. But it wasn't a certainty that seemed to have much power of carrying other certainties with it; indeed it instantly presented one very large puzzle. For the solution of this, Appleby presently applied himself hopefully to his glass of sherry. It wasn't a very reliable ally – a really hot bath was miles better – but he would give it a fair chance.

'Waiter – bring me a bottle of your best champagne!'

This command was uttered so close to Appleby's ear that for a moment he thought he was being addressed. Then he saw that the speaker had sat down – gregariously if somewhat unnecessarily – in the next chair. He had a loose grey skin, and loose grey clothes, and he was now applying himself to the study of a bundle of cables and telegrams. They looked important – and no doubt the problems they presented amply warranted the order their recipient had just given. Appleby returned to his sherry. It was not assisting his mental processes in any way. Perhaps it was the wrong drink.

The champagne arrived with an expedition which almost certainly meant that it would be tepid. The waiter poured a glass in gloomy silence. He clearly disapproved of this exotic behaviour. Then he set the bottle down on a table.

'That's all I want. Take it away and drink it yourself.' The grey man said this in a threatening rather than a cordial voice. 'And see there's another like that waiting for me at dinner. Get?'

The waiter withdrew without vouchsafing any sign that he had got. He was now thoroughly offended.

The grey man watched him go, and then turned to Appleby. 'Moody,' he said.

'Well, yes. I dare say he's had a long day.'

'I said Moody.'

'Oh, I beg your pardon.' Appleby now understood. 'Appleby.'

The grey man nodded with a sort of ferocious cordiality. 'You have some of that champagne, Mr Appleby? We can have it back.'

'No – thank you very much. I've a drink here. Dry sherry.'

The American called Moody glanced at Appleby's glass with suspicion. 'I wouldn't call that safe,' he said. 'I'm on strict orders to drink nothing but champagne. French champagne. Because of my duodenum. Haven't you a duodenum, Mr Appleby?'

'Well, I rather suppose I have – about twelve inches of one. But it never seems particularly to have called for champagne, I'm glad to say. Haven't your doctors given you rather a costly prescription?'

'Huh?'

This, from Moody, appeared to be a sound indicating bafflement. He gave Appleby a long stare which somehow suggested great ability. He might have been a person of the most commanding intellect who has been presented with a philosophical proposition just too remote for comprehension. 'But it does come, you know,' Appleby was prompted to add, 'in half-bottles. Handier for between meals.'

Mr Moody shook his head decisively. 'The corks don't come out right,' he said. 'Not out of the little ones.' He took a sip of champagne, put down the glass, and produced from his waistcoat pocket a small bottle of pills. 'I'm glad you said that about meals,' he went on. 'I have to take these half an hour before. Dangerous to forget. I was warned that way by Dr Cahoon. I go into his clinic every Fall. Come across and look him up, Mr Appleby, if you ever find you have that duodenum after all. I guess you'd like Dr Cahoon's clinic. Most expensive in the United States.'

'I'll certainly bear it in mind.' Appleby felt it was only fair to make a civil response to this gratifying estimate of his financial rating.

Mr Moody swallowed a pill. Then he raised a hand and pointed over Appleby's shoulder. 'That's mine,' he said.

Appleby turned his head. All he could see was the death of General Gordon. 'Is it, indeed?' he said. 'That's most interesting.'

Mr Moody's pointing finger described a semicircle. 'And that's mine too. But there's somebody disputes it, and says it's his.'

This time Mr Moody was indubitably indicating the execution of Queen Mary. Presumably he was the enviable proprietor of the Victorian masterpieces in oils after which these engravings had been made. Appleby tried to think of some apposite question. 'Are they in good condition?' he asked.

Mr Moody had finished his champagne and risen painfully to his feet. He was still clutching his cables, and it appeared that he was proposing to withdraw with them into privacy. 'Condition?' he said. 'Absolutely first-class, Mr Appleby. Soaked in blood. Drenched in it.'

'Blood?' Appleby could only echo this weakly.

'I've gotten a lot of things like that.' Mr Moody nodded – confidentially, mysteriously. 'I've gotten things that nobody knows.'

It wasn't precisely from his sherry that Appleby had to spend a little time sobering up. When he went into the small hotel dining-room he found it crowded, and he was shown to a table already occupied by another diner. This was a middle-aged man who was paying little attention to what he ate, being absorbed in the pages of what appeared to be a magazine. But he closed this when Appleby sat down, and murmured a polite good-evening. Appleby responded – and decided at a glance that his retreat from Urchins had not in fact dispensed him from academic society. This person could only be a don. Appleby glanced at the journal he had set down. It announced itself – in an elegant red type on a grey ground – as *The Review of English Studies*.

One oughtn't to be caught peering at another fellow's reading. But the stranger, following Appleby's glance, smiled amiably. 'It's not *Mind*,' he said, 'and it's not *The Journal of Classical Archeology*. It's not even *Nature*. So I'm afraid I can't offer it to you with the greatest confidence. Still it's pretty good in its way. Certainly as good as my own affair – or perhaps a wee bit better. That's why I keep an eye on it. Of course, our affair is more specialized.'

'You edit a journal, sir?' Appleby asked politely.

'*The Elizabethan and Jacobean Quarterly*. You won't have heard of it.'

'Well, I have – as a matter of fact.' Appleby paused. He found it impossible to believe that the learned person opposite had found his way to the neighbourhood of Urchins at this particular juncture entirely by chance. 'I can't claim to read it regularly. But I have got hold of it from time to time to read papers by an old acquaintance of mine. You probably knew him. Lewis Packford.'

The stranger received this for a moment in silence. He was probably doing much the same sort of thinking as Appleby. 'Yes, of course,' he said presently. 'And Packford's death has been a very shocking thing. Incidentally, there's some extraordinary stuff about it in the evening papers.' He paused. 'My name is Charles Rushout.' He tapped *The Review of English Studies*. 'I try to teach this sort of thing

– or the literature with which it is somewhat tenuously connected – to the young people in the University of Nesfield.'

'How do you do. My name is John Appleby. I am a policeman.'

'How do you do.' Rushout had taken this bald announcement very well. 'Your name, if I may say so, is familiar to me. Am I right in thinking that you run Scotland Yard?'

'My dear Professor, you would be right in thinking that Scotland Yard runs me.'

Rushout smiled – and at the same moment, with an expertness scarcely to be predicted of a scholar, summoned a waiter with the flick of a hand. 'Don't you think,' he asked, 'that we might share a bottle of claret?'

Appleby nodded. 'I have an idea,' he said, 'that we might quite usefully share rather more than that.'

'It isn't this stuff in the evening paper,' Rushout said presently, 'that has brought me down to this part of the world. I'd set out – as you can easily calculate – before that appeared. My first idea was simply to write to Packford's executors. But I suddenly felt, for some reason, most uneasy about this enormously important thing. So I decided to come straight here, and to call on poor Packford's brother in the morning. The suggestion, here in the newspaper, that Packford's death may have been a matter of murder and theft makes me sorry I didn't act sooner. If the book is really lost, it's a calamity.' Rushout applied himself appreciatively to his claret. 'In fact I can't bear to think of it.'

'You interest me very much.' Appleby reached for the bottle and replenished his companion's glass. 'But I ought to say that this report in the paper is in no sense inspired by the police. I'd very much like to know by whom it *was* inspired. If I had the faintest hope that the paper would tell me, I'd be on the line to them now.'

'You mean it may be without substance?' Rushout brightened. 'The book may be safe?'

'There is certainly some substance behind the story. As for the book, it may be safe enough, whatever it is. But I very much doubt it.'

'You don't know about it? You don't know about the *Ecatommiti*?' For a moment Rushout looked surprised. 'But naturally you don't. Packford had, I gather, been dropping hints. But he hadn't come out with it. The paper he intended to send me for the *Elizabethan and Jacobean* was to be the first public word about it.'

'I seem to remember,' Appleby said, 'that the *Ecatommiti* cropped up in a conversation I had with Packford in Italy not very long ago. It's Shakespeare's source for *Othello*?'

'Well – yes and no. It's a collection of yarns put together by an Italian we usually call Cintio, and published in 1565. One of the yarns is the Othello story. But it's never been known whether Shakespeare worked straight from the Italian – a language there's no positive evidence that he knew – or from a translation into French – a language he almost certainly had some knowledge of. Some people have supposed that he must have come across an English version now unknown to us. But Packford had settled the matter – and much more. He'd somehow acquired – I gather from a source in Verona – a copy of the original Italian, copiously annotated by Shakespeare himself. It's the greatest Shakespearian find of the century. Indeed, it sounds to me like the greatest ever.'

'You haven't seen it?'

'No. As far as I know, Packford at the time of his death had shown it to nobody. All I had from him was a letter announcing his discovery and saying that he proposed to send me a paper about it for publication later.'

'It would have been far and away his most sensational contribution to scholarship?'

'Oh, decidedly. I hope it still will be – although it must be a posthumous achievement now… I think there may be another half glass.'

Appleby poured the claret. 'If this book turns up, there is bound to be a tremendous debate whether the annotations are really in Shakespeare's hand?'

'Inevitably.' Rushout chuckled. 'It will keep people busy for years. But Packford, for whose judgement most of us have a vast respect, was quite confident in the matter.'

'Substantial specimens of Shakespeare's hand are extant?'

'Well – yes and no, again. There are signatures. And there is a substantial whack of a manuscript play, quite reasonably to be ascribed to him on literary grounds, in a hand which some of the best authorities declare to be the same that executed the signatures. And Packford declared that the annotations were indistinguishable from either.'

'You gathered that he was excited about the business?'

'Very much so. He did, you know, become tremendously enthusiastic. His letter assured me that the annotations gave a marvellous insight into the mind of the dramatist as he first addressed himself to his material.'

'His enthusiasm might upset his judgement there.'

'I think it very well might. And poor Packford was no literary critic, one is bound to admit. Even if the annotations were quite commonplace – which seems not terribly likely – he would readily convince himself of their profundity. But on the whole scholarly and palaeographical side of the matter he would be very shrewd.'

Appleby was silent for a moment. 'Would you say that Packford,' he then asked, 'was thinking about his discovery at all in terms of money? I happen to know that his affairs were embarrassed – so embarrassed that even he couldn't be unaware of the fact. Didn't his find, if genuine, represent a fortune?'

Rushout drained his glass and nodded. 'Undoubtedly. I haven't, of course, any notion of a figure. But it would be staggering. You know the sort of fancy prices that have been given in the present century for paintings which people have taken it into their heads to declare among the very greatest in the world. I'd suppose this book, although it's only a batch of rather inferior yarns scribbled in by a busy working dramatist, would certainly command money of that order.'

'Don't you think,' Appleby asked, 'that there's something a bit queer about the whole thing? How did Packford come by the book?

If from somebody in Verona, did that somebody know, or didn't he know, what he was selling? If he knew, how did he ever come to part with the thing at any figure Packford could rise to? If he didn't know, how was contact between seller and purchaser ever made? I have it from another source, I may say, that Packford paid a thousand pounds. That seems just wrong, when you come to think about it. It's far too little to have been a reasonable offer to make to an informed person for such a treasure. And it's surely a good deal too much to offer for a copy of Cintio's work if Shakespeare's association with it was unsuspected by the owner.'

'I agree with you. There is a great deal of force in what you say.'

'And there's another puzzle. If Shakespeare really visited Italy, acquired a Cintio, and scribbled in it copiously with the notion of blocking out a play, why did he then leave the book behind him? Wouldn't it have been reasonable to shove it in his luggage and bring it home? Then again, he *did* write a play about Othello. Did he do it from memory?'

Rushout chuckled. 'My dear Sir John, you are starting in on just the sort of questions that all the learned will be asking – supposing that the book is safe and sound, and presently given to the world. There are numerous possible answers. Shakespeare may have visited Italy rather late on in his career, and written *Othello* on the spot. Or he may have gone there as a young man, come across the *Ecatommiti*, scribbled on it and then abandoned it. Later on, and back in England, he may have remembered his abortive interest in the story of the noble Moor, and got hold either of another copy of the Italian or of the French translation of it.'

'Yes, any of these things is possible.' Appleby spoke this time with his eye on the dining-room door. He was awaiting with some curiosity the arrival of Mr Moody for his dinner and his bottle of champagne. 'I ought to tell you,' he said, 'that there are several people at Urchins now who possess a more or less professional interest in our topic. Have you heard of some sort of learned joke about a fellow called Bogdown?'

'I think I have.'

'Well, the members of the Bogdown Society, or whatever it is called, were gathered at Urchins at the time of Packford's death. And they are there still. In addition to which there is Packford's widow, who also belongs to the learned world.'

'A widow?' Rushout was surprised. 'I'd no idea he was married.'

'Nor, till the other day, had anyone else. And that's not entirely the end of the story. But the important people at the moment are those who might take a special interest in Cintio. None of them, so far as I can tell, knows the whole story you have told me. But some of them know quite a lot. Prodger, Limbrick, Rixon. Do these names convey anything to you?'

'Certainly they do. And they would all be very interested indeed.'

Appleby still had his eye on the door. 'And Sankey – does that convey anything?'

'No. I've never heard of him.'

'Prodger had a good deal to say about an American collector called Sankey. But I think he may have got the name wrong. He's been muddled by *Gospel Hymns*.'

'*Gospel Hymns*?'

It was at this moment that Mr Moody entered the dining-room. Appleby indicated him with a swift gesture. 'You wouldn't associate *him* with *Gospel Hymns*?'

Rushout looked quite blank. 'I've never seen him before. And I'm afraid I don't know what you're talking about.'

'That is Moody. Presently he's going to drink champagne. Prodger gets his name wrong, simply because, once upon a time, another Moody collaborated with a Sankey in making a hymn-book. But you, Professor Rushout, know nothing about *this* Moody?'

Rushout hesitated. For a moment, indeed, he seemed thoroughly confused. 'I didn't say that,' he said. 'I only declared that I'd never seen him before. Nor has he ever seen me.'

'May I take it, then, that you have corresponded?'

'Yes.'

Appleby smiled. 'You've told me quite a lot, over this very tolerable claret of ours. Might it be a good idea if you told me a little more?'

The editor of *The Elizabethan and Jacobean Quarterly* received this proposition without enthusiasm. 'Aren't we,' he asked, 'getting on to something quite irrelevant?'

'It certainly isn't irrelevant that the chap over there – who is one of the biggest collectors of this, that and the other thing in America – should be lurking within a few miles of Urchins. That it's irrelevant that you and he have corresponded is something which, of course, you are at liberty to maintain. But perhaps' – and Appleby looked ironically at his companion – 'a moment's further thought will suggest some connexction to you, after all.'

Rushout didn't reply to this. He was glancing with some misgivings at Mr Moody, who was now in process of ordering his dinner. 'You know,' he said rather defensively, 'so many of the great American collectors are highly cultivated men. Indeed, one may confidently say scholarly men. It is a pleasure to have any association with them.'

Appleby smiled. 'I don't doubt it for a moment. In fact, I know several myself. But, just at present, our concern is with the gentleman over there. I'd describe him – well, as belonging to another tradition.'

'He looks deplorable.'

'My dear Professor, that, if I may say so, is a somewhat illiberal and hasty judgement. My own acquaintance with Mr Moody is perhaps also too slight for confident appraisal. But I rather like him.'

'I certainly ought to labour to do so.' Rushout peered rather gloomily into his empty glass. 'For he is, in fact, a benefactor of mine. Not in a personal sense. But – well, he puts up most of the money for *The Elizabethan and Jacobean*. Learned journals, you know, are now uncommonly expensive affairs to finance.'

'That is most enlightened of him. Don't you think, Professor, that you ought to go over and introduce yourself to him? And might I, perhaps, venture to join you for coffee? You and I will have a cognac. Moody, on the orders of Dr Cahoon, will continue to drink champagne.'

Rushout received this suspiciously. 'Don't make fun of me,' he said. 'The position has been a delicate one, as you are perfectly capable of guessing.'

'You mean that Moody's financial aid to the – um – investigating classes hasn't been of an order of the most disinterested?'

'And don't quote Henry James at me.' Rushout grinned with recovered cheerfulness. 'It's not seemly in a policeman.'

'You gave him tips?'

'Just that. As editor of *The Elizabethan and Jacobean*, and with the full agreement of my Advisory Panel – '

'Whatever's that?'

'A collection of impeccably respectable learned persons who are supposed to advise me about my job. With their approval, as I say, I have from time to time given this Moody chap tips. That's to say, when I've had early notice of the turning up of something that might be of interest to a collector, I've let him know.'

'I see. That wouldn't include General Gordon's Bible?'

'General Gordon's Bible?'

'Moody believes himself to own it – together with the prayer-book which Mary Queen of Scots took to the scaffold. Both are satisfactorily drenched in blood. I was puzzled at first, because I thought he was referring to pictures.'

'I didn't know he went in for relics. Beastly things, if you ask me, whether drenched in blood or not. But he has got a tremendous collection of books and manuscripts in the literary field.'

Appleby nodded. 'It sounds as if old Prodger was right in maintaining that Moody – or rather Sankey – was just the man for Packford's big find, and that this fellow Limbrick wouldn't have a chance against him. So I understand you let Moody know about Shakespeare's *Ecatommiti*?'

'In the strictest confidence.' Rushout was again defensive. 'Simply to get him in at the head of the queue. That was more or less the spirit of our agreement.'

'No wonder he's come hurtling across the Atlantic at the news of Packford's death. If he gets the book, I suppose he'll finance your journal for the rest of his days?'

Rushout managed a spirited reply to this. 'If he doesn't', he said, 'he damned well ought to.'

3

DENOUEMENTS AT NIGHT AND IN THE MORNING

Pleasure and action make the hours seem short.
Othello

1

When Appleby got back to Urchins he was shown to his room by the maid who answered the door. His suitcase had been unpacked and his bed turned down; it continued to be evident that the place had a smooth domestic routine which hadn't been disturbed by the untoward events recently taking place in it. The night was mild, and Appleby spent a few minutes by the open window, smoking a cigarette and staring out into the darkness. The ground must fall away here, for there were a few sleepy yellow lights low down in the middle distance. It suddenly seemed a very short time ago since he had been gazing into quite a different darkness, with Lewis Packford beside him and the waters of Garda invisible below. There hadn't been any mystery then. Or rather – Appleby thought – there had been, but he had lacked the alertness to mark the fact. It was deplorably true that, as a detective, he had a certain leeway to make up.

Which was a good reason, he told himself, for getting on with the job now. He put out his cigarette and left the bedroom. It was almost at the end of a long corridor – one corresponding, he supposed, to the downstairs corridor along which he had been conducted that morning. He was stepping into this when he became aware of another door opening a little farther down. It was the manner in which this was happening that arrested him. For the door was being opened from within, and inch by inch. He was in the presence of extreme nervousness and caution – and of these qualities exercising themselves in a manner not very effectively controlled by intelligence.

If one wants to reconnoitre the outer world from inside a room, one's best plan is to act swiftly. A door briskly opened and briskly shut again attracts little attention. A door opening in very slow motion is something that most people become aware of at once.

Appleby stepped back into the darkness of his room, leaving his own door a little ajar. Probably what he was witnessing was something of no great significance. There are people for whom other people's rooms hold a compulsive fascination, and the phenomenon known as 'just taking a peep' is of not uncommon occurrence in miscellaneous house-parties. Still, he had better make sure. He had better both mark who this was emerging, and then discover whose room was being emerged from.

It was Mrs Husbands. For a moment Appleby was disposed to conclude that this was very much a mare's nest. Nobody at Urchins, presumably, had a better title to move from room to room than the housekeeper. And if there was something a little odd in her manner of performing this commonplace task, that might simply be because recent events had badly shaken her nerve. She might, for instance, have become subject to irrational fears, and have taken her preliminary survey of the corridor in order to reassure herself that she wasn't being stalked by somebody with a gun.

Only it wasn't like that. Appleby had to take only a glance at the woman as she now stood revealed to realize that any such explanation of her conduct and condition was totally inadequate. The corridor was brightly lit, and her features as well as her posture were clearly distinguishable. Mrs Husbands was breathing fast; she was as pale as the wall behind her; and her eyes glittered with what might have been either excitement or fear. Even when one remembered that she rather went in for putting on emotional turns, her present bearing in the apparent solitude of this corridor was sufficiently striking. But now she seemed to brace herself, and Appleby heard her taking a single deep breath. Then she looked quickly in either direction, walked quickly but rather unsteadily to a staircase, and disappeared.

Appleby stepped back into the corridor and moved towards the room from which Mrs Husbands had appeared. It wasn't necessary to suppose that it was empty; what Mrs Husbands had emerged from might be some harrowing or alarming interview. She might even have found another dead body, complete with a valedictory message still wet upon a postcard... Appleby checked himself before this irresponsible fancy. He would knock at the door. If there was a summons to enter, he would stick his head in, identify the occupant, and excuse himself on the score of unfamiliarity with the house. If there was no reply, he would simply walk in and look around.

But this plan didn't come off. His hand was raised to knock, when a voice spoke reproachfully behind him. 'Oh, hullo! Why didn't you come in to dinner?'

He turned round. It was Alice who had somehow appeared just behind him, and she was now looking at him with frank curiosity. 'I went out to the local,' he said.

'I can't say I blame you.' Alice gave a large unashamed yawn. Then, seeming to remember that this was somewhat unrefined, she gave another, imitation, one with a rosy hand elegantly raised to her lips. 'Oh, my,' she said, 'wouldn't it be lovely to go to bed!'

'Well – why not?' Appleby wasn't sure, as he heard himself say this, that it didn't contain an undesirable ambiguity. 'Why don't you?' he amended.

'It wouldn't be polite – not before a quarter past ten.' Alice spoke with confidence; this must be something that she had read in a manual of such matters. 'But – I say – I know where we can get a drink. And without anybody knowing.'

Appleby wasn't convinced that this was polite either. But he allowed himself to be led downstairs and into what proved to be the library. The little mystery of Mrs Husbands, he had decided, could wait. A private word with Alice mightn't be without its usefulness.

'Over on that table, they are.' Alice sat down with aplomb. She knew when it was the business of a gentleman to dispense refreshment. 'I'm leaving,' she said suddenly. 'Tomorrow, first thing. And they won't find me in a hurry, either.'

Appleby poured drinks. 'You've had enough?'

'More than enough. I can't understand what they talk about, and I don't want to. Tonight was the worst of the lot. I'm going after breakfast, I am. And please don't come after me.'

Appleby laughed. 'The police, you mean? I don't expect they'll want to.'

'And not the lawyers either. That Mr Rood, for instance. I don't like him. I don't like him at all. And I don't want his money.'

Appleby was startled. 'Rood's been offering you money?'

'Well, Loo's money. Loo had written something extra, saying that I was to have £5,000. And I won't take it. It makes me angry to think about it.'

'It's certainly not very much.' Appleby thought he ought to be soothing and persuasive. 'But perhaps, when you consider that his affairs haven't been going well – '

Alice nodded vigorously. 'That's just it. Mr Rood has explained about the will. Edward was to have this house, and the rents from the farms and places. But it won't be enough – not to keep a gentleman's place the way it ought to be. And everything else goes to Ruth. But that won't be much, either.'

'I see.' Alice's processes of mind, Appleby thought, were never predictable. 'But you know, if that's how it is, Ruth's share is bound to be very much more than £5,000. Besides, she earns money from her job.'

'They *pay* her?' Alice was astonished. 'For talking all that stuff about who Thomas Horscroft was?'

'Certainly.'

'I call that queer – I do. But I won't have that £5,000, all the same. I oughtn't ever to have been more than a bit of fun – not to Loo. I must have got ideas – don't you think – for poor Loo almost to have married me, and then to have written in about all that money. But they can't make me take it – can they? – if they don't even know where I am.'

'Obviously not, Alice. But you can't refuse the money without disappearing, you know. And I think you really want to disappear for quite a different reason. This sort of place, and these sort of people bore you stiff. Don't they, now?'

'Of course they do.' There was a hint of a tear on Alice's exquisite cheek. 'I'd give my eyes to be back in a nice superior corner of the trade at this minute.'

'Then back you go.'

Alice looked at Appleby round-eyed. 'I really can?'

'There's nothing in the world to prevent you. If we *do* want you, we'll find you, all right. You know that as well as I do. Meanwhile, if you cut out of it, my dear, you'll be doing a very sensible thing. By the way, didn't you try to cut out of it before? And with – um – Loo?'

'Cut out of it with Loo?' She looked at him in perplexity. 'What do you mean?'

'On that very first night? Be honest, Alice. Didn't you try to persuade him to make a run for it with you?'

'Of course not!' Alice was indignant. 'I was much too cross with him. I don't know what I wanted – or what I did, or what I said. I just don't remember. But of course I didn't try to take him away. This was his own house, wasn't it?'

'Have you lost anything since you came to Urchins, Alice?'

'Only my temper once or twice. And who wouldn't do that, among such a lot? I ask you!'

'I rather agree. But you're sure you haven't missed anything? Nothing in the way of personal property?'

Alice looked suddenly rather frightened. 'I don't know what you mean,' she said.

Appleby shook his head. 'When somebody uses those words, my child, it's ten to one that he or she means just the opposite. You have missed something, haven't you?'

'Well, yes. But nothing important. It's just something that that cook, or one of the girls, has taken, I suppose. You can't expect everybody to be honest all the time, can you? It just isn't life, that isn't.'

'Perhaps, it's not. But you haven't mentioned this loss to anyone?'

'Certainly not!' Alice was again indignant. 'That wouldn't be refined. Not when you're a guest in a gentleman's private residence. It would be different in a hotel. But I never like hearing of that sort of thing – complaints of pilfering, I mean. There's nothing gives licensed premises a worse name. And it would be dead common to complain about such a thing, when you're in a country seat.'

Appleby chuckled. 'I'd have missed some rather interesting inquiries in my time, Alice, if that particular rule of good society had been observed. But let's not bother more about it now. You get off to bed – and pack as soon as you get up in the morning. Now I must go and see Edward.'

'You'll find him in that funny little room of his, I think. But I can really go in the morning? I shan't be wanted for more of the – mystery?'

Appleby shook his head – seriously, this time. 'The morning is still quite a long time off,' he said. 'And I'm beginning to hope the mystery won't last far into it.'

2

Edward Packford looked up as Appleby entered the little room. For a moment he didn't appear to recognize his visitor. And for a moment, too, Appleby had once more the odd sensation of seeing a Lewis Packford who had, as it were, shrunk in the wash. Indeed, this time the effect was even more striking, for there was something shrivelled or diminished about Edward; he seemed not quite the man who had greeted Appleby that morning.

'I'm afraid,' Appleby said, 'that your solicitor's news hasn't been too good?'

'My solicitor?' Edward frowned – abstractedly, as if his mind were still rather far away. 'Rood isn't my solicitor. And it's a pity he was Lewis'.'

'He mismanaged things? I understand his claim to be that he was very little consulted over money matters.'

'It may have been so, Sir John. I don't know much about it.' Edward Packford had drawn forward a chair with automatic punctiliousness. But he appeared indisposed to talk freely.

'Would you say that your brother had confidence in him?'

There was a marked silence. Edward for some reason seemed to find this question hard to answer. 'Did Lewis have confidence in him?' he repeated. 'I believe that, in some ways, he had. But he used to laugh at him – not as a lawyer, but as a would-be scholar. And he used to put on a turn.'

'A turn?' Appleby was puzzled.

'Lewis was rather good at mimicry. He used to put on a turn – imitating this fellow Rood rolling his umbrella. I expect Rood resented it.'

Appleby looked at Edward curiously. 'What makes you think that?'

Edward frowned again, as if the question irked or puzzled him. 'He expresses himself in a kind of gloating way. No – that's not quite right. He makes remarks that in themselves express ordinary decent feelings. But he takes care that they sound quite forbiddingly unconcerned and conventional.'

Appleby nodded. 'I noticed that in him almost at once. But it may be no more than a mannerism. And I'd say that Rood has ability.'

'No doubt.' Edward appeared uninterested.

'But you're more concerned with the fellow's news than with the fellow himself? And money's going to be tight?'

'Certainly it is. There's a widow to provide for. To say nothing of a mistress.' Edward produced rather a grim smile. 'The jointure for a mistress is apparently £5,000.'

'You'd quarrel with that?'

'Of course not.' Edward spoke sharply. 'If Lewis found the girl worth going to bed with, she must have whatever sum he named.'

'Even if she's not worth it?'

Quite unexpectedly, Edward Packford smiled. 'But she is worth it. You know that as well as I do. If I were quite a different man from what I happen to be, I'd be prepared to write a big cheque for the privilege of having slept with Alice. Or so I suppose. But of course that's all damned nonsense. The point is that the girl's a good sort of girl anyway. Let her take her £5,000 and depart. I'm sure we bore her most horribly.'

Appleby laughed. 'As it happens, I know that to be only too true. But she won't take the money. She thinks it ought to go either to Ruth – for having beaten her, I suppose, to the altar – or to you, my dear sir, in order to enable you to maintain what she calls a country seat.'

'Well, that's very handsome of her, and bears out what I said. But I don't know that £5,000 will go far in the way of patching up

Urchins. Not, Sir John, that matters of that sort are at all your business.'

'I assure you that I can't help taking an interest in them.' Appleby said this rather drily. 'And I suppose that the real mischief is your brother's having contracted a valid marriage as well as a bogus one. How do you feel about Ruth?'

'Feel about her?' Edward, who had been prowling restlessly round his small room, turned round impatiently. 'Am I called on to have any feeling about the woman – whether the one way or the other?' He stared queerly at Appleby – queerly, since his gaze seemed to be directed upon something quite different and quite absorbing which he was viewing through Appleby as through a window. 'She's all right, I suppose – although I think we agreed she wasn't precisely the dream-woman for either of us.' Edward laughed – and his laughter, more than his speech, brought it home to Appleby that he was in some quite abnormal state. It seemed certain that the new owner of Urchins did tremendously care about the place, and that Rood's disclosure of the full precariousness of the position had shocked him profoundly. This, at least, was the best way of accounting for his condition.

'I'm not sure myself,' Appleby said, 'whether Ruth improves more on acquaintance or just impresses more on acquaintance. It's not by any means the same thing.'

'It would be idle to maintain that I greatly care to find out. She was good enough for Lewis – although it's true the fact might be more impressive if he hadn't almost immediately made a fool of himself with this other girl. And so, I suppose, she's good enough for me – as my brother's widow. It isn't, one supposes, a very close relationship.'

'You'd say that, after this clandestine and rather tenuous marriage, she's fully entitled to her share of his property?'

'Of course she is. She's entitled to anything she has a reasonable expectation of. Let her take it, and depart in charity.'

There was another silence. Appleby devoted it to wondering just what it was in Edward that now so acutely puzzled him. Was there some whole aspect of the man which, earlier that day, had escaped him? Or since then had something transforming occurred which Appleby himself hadn't tumbled to or got into focus? Certainly he found himself strangely in the dark with Edward now. And into his head there floated – utterly incongruously, as it seemed – the image of Alice on a lamentable occasion; the image of Alice being suddenly hit on the head with a bottle by that perfectly respectable person who had the habit of dropping in to listen to the nine o'clock news. It was just such an impression that Edward, somehow, now gave. He might have been hit over the head with a bottle no more than ten minutes ago. The ten minutes was important in the picture. For it wasn't from something revealed to him some hours ago that the man was suffering now. Almost immediately before he himself had entered this room – Appleby found himself grotesquely convinced – Edward Packford had been hit on the head with a bottle. And his assailant, it was possible to feel, had borne an appearance as respectable as Alice's had done.

But all this didn't seem particularly helpful, and Appleby decided to move on to other matters. 'I came in,' he said, 'to give you several pieces of news. And the first of them takes us back to Rood. So far as I'm concerned, he was the first man to advance a number of notions which decidedly deserve chewing over still. And one of them we may regard as now verified. Your brother did acquire in Italy – whether in Verona or elsewhere – a literary document of the greatest importance. Unless he was all wrong – your brother, I mean, not Rood – he had got hold of an Italian book quite copiously and very significantly annotated by Shakespeare. But perhaps this isn't news to you, after all?'

'It's news, all right.' Edward spoke slowly, and for the first time in their interview there was something in his voice that carried simple and unenigmatic conviction. 'Of course, Lewis seems to have been dropping hints to that learned crew of his about something pretty remarkable. But it might quite well have been remarkable only to scholars. Whereas, unless my sense of these things is badly astray, what you are telling me is big news in a purely practical and mundane sense.'

'Precisely. Your brother had possessed himself of something worth a very large sum of money.'

Edward, still prowling around his room, turned and looked at Appleby steadily. 'And then he was killed.'

'So you say. So Rood said. So some others appear to think. So part of the apparent evidence makes it very difficult to believe.' Appleby paused on this succinct statement. 'And to all this we must add that nobody appears to know where that immensely valuable book is now. But we do appear to know whose legal property it is, if and when it turns up.'

'Certainly we do. It's Ruth's.' Edward could not have made this statement in a tone that was more matter of fact. 'By the way, may I ask you how you have come by this fresh knowledge?'

'From a fellow called Charles Rushout.'

Edward shook his head. 'I've never heard of him.'

'He's a Professor of Literature in some northern university or other. He edits a journal called *The Elizabethan and Jacobean Quarterly*. And I found him at your local hotel this evening, all agog to present himself to you and tell you of the immense treasure which Urchins at present so unsuspectingly enshrines.'

'How does he come to know about it?'

'Your brother wrote and told him. Later, your brother was going to send him a paper for his journal, announcing and describing his discovery. But that's not quite all. Rushout's first action on hearing the news was to pass it on quietly to an American collector called Moody. And Moody's now at your local hotel, too.'

This time, Edward did really appear to be staggered. But he still spoke quietly. 'What sort of a collector? A college librarian – that sort of fellow?'

'Not at all that sort of fellow. Shrewd, ignorant, vastly rich, and in the grip of some advanced acquisitive mania.'

'Does he keep on swallowing pills for the benefit of his duodenum?'

'Well, yes – he does.' Appleby was surprised. 'You know him?'

'Dear me, no. But I've heard Lewis talk about him. I'd forgotten his name. But that's right – Moody.'

Appleby laughed. 'He's the fellow, in fact, that Prodger consistently refers to as Sankey, and baits Limbrick with.'

'No doubt. And I've heard Lewis tell some queer yarns about him. You think Moody is proposing to come along and make an offer for this book if it can be found? Ruth must be told at once. It's her affair, and it's obviously of the greatest importance. What's this book called?'

'It's the *Ecatommiti* of Cintio – or perhaps part of the *Ecatommiti*, I'm not quite sure. It isn't a thing I've ever set eyes on. But Ruth herself will know about it, since it's her line of country too. And Rushout, of course, will be able to describe it accurately.'

'Good.' Edward had become brisk and incisive. 'We must have a thorough hunt for it tomorrow. It may, of course, have been stolen. In fact, we can't blink the high probability that it has been. On the other hand, it may conceivably just be lying about. Lewis, as you perhaps know, could be almost incredibly careless about such things. Do you think it had dawned on him, by the way, that this *Ecatommiti* was not only his final passport to fame but also potentially his absolute financial salvation?'

Appleby shook his head. 'I can't possibly tell. But my guess is that he hadn't focused that second aspect of the thing at all.'

'Well, that makes it the more probable that he simply did leave it lying about. He may conceivably have left it lying about so carelessly that the thief – if there was a thief – was baffled after all. Do you think that's possible?'

'Yes, I do. And I have a notion somebody else does, as well.'

3

It was eleven o'clock when Appleby knocked at the door through which he had earlier seen Mrs Husbands so oddly emerge. The whole household seemed to have gone to bed, so he wasn't surprised when he got a reply from within. He opened the door and entered. The occupant was Mr Rood.

The solicitor was standing in front of a suitcase, fishing out a pair of pyjamas. He turned and looked at Appleby with sombre distaste. 'Ah, Sir John,' he said. 'I am very glad to see you. For a word in private, that is to say. For I must confess that I am still very much dissatisfied. However, it is something that the matter is now in your hands. I hope you have come to agree that the police didn't, in the first instance, get to the bottom of the matter.'

'Yes, I have.' Appleby sat down. 'And I must tell you at once that certain of your suspicions, at least, have been substantiated. Packford did undoubtedly procure in Italy something not only of the greatest scholarly interest but of a very large monetary value as well.' Appleby gave a brief account of the Cintio. 'So that's what the thousand pounds went for, we must presume. And it was a wonderful bargain, you'll agree.'

'Most interesting,' Rood said. 'And I fear that our late friend's secretive disposition was fatal to him. Had he divulged the nature of his find to myself or any other competent person, it would have been represented to him that such a treasure should be kept in the strong-room of his bank. As it was, he was shot and robbed. It is all most distressing.' Rood unfolded the pyjamas and laid them neatly on the bed. 'But there is the faked suicide, Sir John. That was a false step, surely, on the murderer's part. It gives us a vital piece of information – one which enormously narrows the field. I regret that I cannot offer you a cigarette. I never smoke.'

'Thank you, I've finished smoking for the night. And I think I know what you mean. If the words written on that postcard were indeed a forgery – as I know you believe – then the field is certainly narrowed. It's no use looking outside the circle of those who could produce such a thing. But aren't you neglecting another possibility? If Packford himself wrote those words, either upon quite a different occasion, or there and then but with no notion that he was going to die, then the situation is quite different. There's an open field. And now consider another point. You mentioned his secretive disposition. But if he was murdered simply that somebody might steal and market this book, then it is surely probable that its very great value was known to the murderer beforehand. So who could have known? At what point did the secretiveness break down? I came upon one answer this evening.'

Rood looked suddenly sharply curious. 'Here at Urchins?'

'No, not at Urchins. Everybody here seems to have known that Packford had made *some* important discovery; and I have indeed some evidence of an awareness that this perhaps implied the presence of an enormously valuable article somewhere here in the house. But what I'm speaking of is something different. Usually, I seem to remember, Packford saved up his more important discoveries for a book. This time he decided on a learned journal. He wrote a preliminary letter, stating just what he believed he'd found, to a man called Rushout. You've heard of him?'

'Certainly.' Rood sounded offended. 'I take a considerable interest, you know, in the field of scholarship with which we are involved. Rushout edits *The Elizabethan and Jacobean*.'

'Exactly. So there is one man who knew, well before Packford died, just what Packford had got hold of. And there's another. For Rushout passed on the information – I fear not entirely properly – to an American collector called Moody.'

'Moody? God bless my soul!'

'I see you know something about him too. But what you probably don't know is that both Rushout and Moody are within a couple of miles of us at this moment.'

'You greatly surprise me, Sir John.' Rood contrived his usual effect of implying that he really wasn't surprised at all. 'It bears out the adage,' he added, 'that one ought be prepared for all eventualities.'

'No doubt. Certainly we must be prepared to see both these people turn up at Urchins tomorrow morning: Rushout to represent confidentially to Edward Packford the very great value of something conceivably just lying about the house, and Moody to flourish a cheque-book far, far bigger than our compatriot Limbrick's.'

'I presume you have told Edward Packford about this, Sir John?'

'Certainly. And I understood he was going to tell his sister-in-law before he went to bed. He at once pointed out that the Cintio, being simply part of his brother's personal property, would go to her.'

Rood nodded. 'That is incontestable. And he realizes, I suppose, that this book is likely to be worth more than Urchins itself and everything else it contains?'

'I'm sure he does. And he too, by the way, has heard of Moody. His brother, it seems, had anecdotes about him.'

'I can well believe it, Sir John. As a collector, Moody might be described as notorious rather than distinguished. Still the cheque-book is there. Should the book turn up, I doubt whether Mrs Packford will get as good a price in any other quarter.'

'What do you think of Mrs Husbands?'

'Mrs Husbands?' If Rood was startled by this abrupt question he did nothing to betray the fact. 'I cannot say that I have ever addressed my mind to the subject of our late friend's housekeeper. What she says of the ink on that postcard I suspect of being nonsense. Apart from that, she seems an entirely competent person. And she gets a small legacy.'

'Only a small one? She has clearly been very much affected by her employer's death; and I have wondered whether the connection might be a close or long-standing affair. You have had no private conversation with her?'

'Dear me, no.' Rood appeared to be genuinely surprised. 'But of course I will have a word with her before I leave. That will be only civil.'

Appleby got up to go. He had learnt something during this little interview – although it hadn't been precisely from Rood's conversation. 'And when in fact are you leaving?' he asked.

'It was my intention to leave quite early tomorrow morning. But now I think I shall venture to stay rather longer.' Rood gave his singularly mirthless smile. 'Yes, I think I shall make so bold as to stop on till lunch-time. You say that Rushout and Moody will be coming to Urchins. Rushout I already know. But I should like to make the acquaintance of Moody, and I don't mind a later train. One's plans should always be flexible, as I think I have remarked before. Moody, from all accounts, is not perhaps a person to admit to one's intimacy without a good deal of thought. But a short chat is another matter. I shall certainly have that with him.'

At half-past eleven Appleby entered the library. It was a modestly unobtrusive entry, effected only with the aid of a tiny pencil of light from a pocket torch. He picked up a couple of cushions from a chair, climbed the spiral staircase, and seated himself in as comfortable a fashion as he could contrive in the small gallery. It afforded an excellent view – or would have done so, had there been anything but a pit of darkness beneath him. He had always had a fancy, he told himself, for the front row of the dress circle. Only on this occasion there was no very definite promise that the curtain would go up. He was fairly sure that there had been a performance on at least one previous night. But it mightn't repeat itself now. There are some activities which tend to be inhibited by the presence of the police in the house.

And in any case he would probably have a wait of an hour or two. To a marauding mind it is the small hours that seem most secure. It wouldn't do not to take up his own position early – but it almost certainly meant a long and unentertaining vigil. He had kept a good many of them in the past, and sometimes in positions vastly more uncomfortable than this. No doubt it was wholesome a little to renew his youth in this fashion… Somewhere in the house a clock struck midnight. And it had scarcely ceased when there was a sound below. The library door had opened.

Appleby felt a faint shiver run down his spine. Yes – it was like old days. Not, it was true, like any of the old star occasions – but certainly like quite a number of endearingly humdrum ones… A light had now been flicked on down below: the soft light of a single reading-lamp. Well, you could call that curtain-up. He himself was still securely shrouded in shadow. He leant forward to distinguish the play.

It was – somewhat against his expectation – old Professor Prodger who held the stage. He was swathed in a thick woollen dressing-gown. Viewed from this angle, his bald head set above his white beard suggested a large poached egg. He was standing in the middle of the floor and appeared to be pointing at one of the rows of bookshelves. So decided was this impression that Appleby peered round the library in search of a second intruder whose gaze Prodger might be directing in this way. But then Prodger's hand and extended finger moved in a series of short jerks. He was counting. And presently, having achieved this to his satisfaction, he toddled over to a particular shelf and began taking down the books and examining them one by one.

Well, that was that. That precisely such a process had been going on in Lewis Packford's library lately had been the conjecture formed by Appleby as a consequence of his own careful inspection of the shelves. But Prodger was somehow a surprise. However, he was now going to receive a surprise himself. Appleby was about to lean forward from the gallery and address the venerable person below, when he saw Prodger suddenly straighten himself and turn round.

He had clearly heard something to alarm him from outside the room. The next moment, and with astonishing agility, he had reached over the back of a sofa to the reading-lamp and plunged the library back into darkness. A bare second later, the door opened.

Appleby chuckled to himself. Perhaps it was Edward Packford. Perhaps it was the vigilant Mrs Husbands. In any case, it would be amusing to see Prodger detected and embarrassingly exposed… Again a light flicked on. It was the same subdued light from the same lamp. Prodger, by some continued gymnastic skill, had contrived to vanish. In the middle of the room – also in pyjamas and dressing-gown – stood Canon Rixon. He looked more extravagantly ugly than ever, so that Appleby found himself wondering whether so villainous an appearance was really compatible with the elevated moral character which its owner in all other regards seemed to evince. Appleby was just recalling this as an issue which had been raised in an interesting context by Socrates, when the room below him once more vanished abruptly into darkness. Rixon had acted precisely as had Prodger – and presumably for the same reason. A third visitor was turning up.

This time it was Limbrick – who had rather been the subject of Appleby's expectation in the first place. And Limbrick was bolder. He switched on the main lights in the library, so that Appleby had hastily to edge himself more securely out of sight. But it was possible to see that Rixon was now as invisible as Prodger – and that Limbrick had gone straight to a far corner of the room and begun the same sort of examination as Prodger had been engaged upon when interrupted.

Limbrick worked in silence, and in silence Appleby regarded him. The whole situation was like something in a farce – a farce that has gone hopelessly wrong and is playing itself to a mute and baffled theatre. Prodger and Rixon were presumably cowering behind some of the larger pieces of furniture, and each proposing so to remain until he had the library to himself again. But that looked as if it might be a long time. Limbrick had the air of a man who means serious business, and there was no reason to suppose that he mightn't work till dawn. For there could be very little doubt about what all this was in aid of. Without perhaps knowing specifically what they were looking for, each was cherishing the hope that Lewis Packford's last and most enigmatical discovery was something that could be run to earth carelessly thrust away between one book and another. It was a supposition that squared quite well with much in the known habits of the dead man. But Appleby thought rather poorly, all the same, of the chances of these devoted and nocturnal researchers. And he didn't feel that he himself was, after all, learning very much. It might be a good idea if the audience now gave the players a token round of applause and then went off to bed. Appleby was just about to make himself heard to this effect when there was a fresh development. Once more the library door had opened – this time without any preliminary awareness on the part of the intruder already holding the field. And the person who appeared framed in it was Alice.

A second later, Limbrick turned and became aware of her. 'Oh, hullo,' he said coolly. 'What are you doing here, my girl?'

'I'm looking for something.'

Alice, who had not undressed, said this in a perfectly commonplace way. Nevertheless Appleby leaned sharply forward to get a better view of her. And Limbrick, too, seemed to look at her with closer attention. He returned a book to its shelf. 'Looking for something? Well, so am I, so we can count ourselves in the same boat. And just what are you looking for, may I ask?'

'I don't know.'

Limbrick laughed rather uneasily. 'Don't you, indeed? I'd suppose that to be rather unusual. But it applies, oddly enough, to myself. I'm damned if I know what I'm looking for. However, I shall know it when I see it – if I'm not a greater fool than I suppose myself. So go about your business, my dear, and leave me alone. I don't mind your poking around, as long as you don't make a row.' He made to turn back to the shelves, and then paused. 'Are *you* going to recognize what you're looking for, when *you* see it?'

'I don't know that either.' This time, Alice's voice was troubled. She looked round the room. 'Is this,' she asked, 'a public library, or something?'

'What's that?' Limbrick laid down another book and looked at her sharply. 'Have you been drinking? Or are you just being damned silly?'

'That isn't a thing any gentleman ought to say to a lady.' Alice was angry, and she had raised her voice. 'No perfect gentleman would say that about drinking.'

'Be quiet! Do you want to wake the whole house, you little idiot?'

What next happened was surprising. Alice had moved, in a curiously hesitant fashion, to a table upon which stood a small bronze statuette. Now she picked this up and threw it at Limbrick, with astonishing force. It flew past his head and crashed into a shelf of books beyond. Thwarted in this attack, she was looking round for another missile – and Limbrick, correspondingly, seemed to be preparing to make a rush at her – when Appleby called out loudly but calmly from his gallery. 'That will do, I think. Alice, sit down and be quiet. Limbrick, stay where you are.'

'And now, I wonder if you'd all emerge?' Appleby had come down the spiral staircase and placed himself close to Alice. He turned to Limbrick. 'You've had quite an audience, you know. Prodger, for instance. Professor, may we have a word with you?'

This summons was obeyed. Very composedly, Prodger emerged from behind a stack of books at the end of the room. He had a pair of spectacles on his nose and was carrying a bulky volume. 'Did I hear voices?' he asked mildly. 'Dear me, Dr Appleby! You too, perhaps, have the habit of nocturnal research. There is much to be said for it. There is a great deal to be said for it. The quiet of the night is conducive to concentration, is it not?' He held up his book. 'I have been refreshing my mind on the subject of conditional-concessive clauses in Old English prose. An important topic – but intricate, undeniably intricate.' He paused. 'But do I see Limbrick? Pilfering,

I presume. Looking round, I should judge, for some small and unconsidered trifle to carry off as a memorial of our poor friend Packford. One of the rarer quarto editions, perhaps, of an Elizabethan play. A thing eminently convenient to slip into the pocket. Well, well. Well, well, well!' Prodger made his guinea-pig's noise. 'And now I suppose we ought to go to bed.'

'We ought certainly to do so quite soon,' Appleby said. 'But first, perhaps, we should conduct a little more research into what you call nocturnal researching. Dr Rixon, might it not be a good idea if you were to join us?'

Canon Rixon had been behind a sofa, and this was so placed that his emergence had to be on all fours. But he seemed no more perturbed than Prodger had been. 'I haven't found it,' he said. 'But perhaps it doesn't greatly matter. Perhaps we can rely on the discretion of whatever person it falls into the hands of. Alice, my dear, you look a little strained. I think it might be as well to get you off to sleep. You will feel much better in the morning. So, for that matter, shall we all.'

'Do I understand,' Appleby asked, 'that you came down to hunt for a recent and very valuable acquisition of the late Lewis Packford's, Dr Rixon? And, if so, was it – well, discreet?'

'It would have been most indiscreet, had I been doing anything of the sort, Sir John. But my quest was for something quite different. I believe you have heard about Bogdown?'

'The imaginary antiquarian you all had some joke about? Well, yes – I have.'

'I judged that it would be just as well to possess myself of our transactions. The transactions, that is to say, of the Bogdown Society. They were in poor Packford's keeping. Judged strictly as a matter of private diversion, they are not unentertaining. But there is undeniably an element of lampoon in them. They make injudiciously free, in places, with the names and reputations of some of our colleagues. Publicized in any way, they might occasion pain. Which would be deplorable, would it not? So I decided to look round for them, here in poor Packford's library, and remove them into safe-keeping. And, naturally, it wasn't a matter with which I wanted to trouble our present host.'

'What pitiful twaddle!' Limbrick had taken a step forward and spoken indignantly. 'Isn't it perfectly clear that we've all been caught out neatly by this confounded policeman?' He gestured contemptuously at Appleby. 'Isn't it undeniable that we've all been nosing after whatever it is that Packford has come up with? Unless a thief has got away with it – '

'Don't you mean,' Appleby asked mildly, 'unless a thief has *already* got away with it?'

'I simply mean that Packford had certainly got hold of something enormously important. Everything he hinted at showed that – and he was no fool in such matters. And, if it's still about, there's a damned good chance that it's simply shoved in somewhere on these shelves. He'd think that safe enough, and know just where to lay his hands on it. I'm so certain it's a big thing that I'd buy every book in this room to get hold of it – as I told his wife this afternoon. But I'd like to get my nose into it first, all the same. And so would you two.' Limbrick waved a hand at Prodger and Rixon. 'But what this girl's after – if she hasn't simply taken leave of her senses – beats me. And now I'm going to bed.'

Limbrick turned and marched from the room. Appleby watched him go. 'I see no good reason,' he said, 'why you gentlemen shouldn't follow our friend's example. I think I can promise the Bogdown Papers, or whatever they are called, won't cause any embarrassment to the learned world. And perhaps, Professor, you could take the conditional-concessive clauses with you. I'd like to have a word with Alice.'

'Quite so, quite so.' Prodger nodded cheerfully. 'But my investigation is, in fact, concluded. The matter is intricate, as I say – but I am fairly confident that I now have a good grasp of it. Which is satisfactory. It is also satisfactory that Limbrick – whom I have always distrusted, as you know – should have been unmasked. Good night, good night.' Prodger toddled to the door. 'Or ought one to say good morning?' He paused expectantly, got no reply, and went out with a final vague nod.

Canon Rixon gave a benevolent sigh. 'Poor Prodger!' he said. 'I fear he is beginning to show the burden of his years. At times, however, he remains remarkably shrewd. And old age – although it is a sad thing to admit – often has its unscrupulous side. I am only too afraid that Prodger's actual aims in this library tonight were identical with those of Limbrick.'

'Are you, indeed?' Appleby allowed himself no more than a mild irony in this.

'And now, my dear Sir John, I wonder whether I might not myself be the better person to have a little talk with our friend Alice? She and I are in a relation of confidence, I am happy to think. And then I can see the dear girl to bed.'

'If she isn't in a state to see herself to bed, I shall call Mrs Husbands.' Appleby now spoke briskly. 'If you want to have a talk with her, it had better be at breakfast. Because she's going to be off shortly afterwards.'

'That's right.' During the whole of these exchanges Alice had sat curiously limp and mute. But now she sat up and spoke with energy. 'I'm leaving, I am.' She turned to Appleby. 'Not that the Reverend hasn't been nice to me – in an old gentleman's fatherly way, if you know what I mean. But none of them thinks I was really right for Loo.'

'This is very sad.' Rixon moved to the door. 'But I hope, my dear Alice, that I may be able to see you now and then. There is, I judge, no impropriety in a clergyman's visiting a tavern from time to time. Positive frequentation is, of course, another matter. Good night, my dear. Good night, Sir John. I am confident that I can leave that delicate little matter of our transactions to your discretion.'

'Would you describe yourself as all right again?' Appleby had turned to Alice as Rixon left the room.

'Yes, thank you.'

'You know that you've been chucking things around?'

'Chucking things around? Come off it!' Alice was indignant. 'I wouldn't think of such a thing. Not in a gentleman's seat, I wouldn't.'

Appleby walked across the library and picked up the statuette. 'You nearly got Limbrick's head,' he said. 'With this. You might have knocked him out. Do I understand you remember nothing about it?'

'Nothing at all.' Alice was frightened and subdued. 'It must have come over me again. I just know I went upstairs to bed.'

'Well, as you can see, you came down again. You came down to look for something.'

'It would be my travelling-case, that Loo gave me.'

'Exactly. You've been worrying about it, as I discovered before.' Appleby paused. 'You've really no idea where it is?'

'Of course I haven't.' Alice managed to speak again with some spirit. 'I wouldn't be behaving queer about it if I did.'

'It's in the boot of Lewis Packford's car. I think you put it there yourself. I think, Alice, you really did have a shot at taking him away – quite a resolute shot. But you don't remember it. Because it happened when you were upset. Perhaps when you were very upset indeed.' Appleby carried the statuette across the room and replaced it on its table. There was no sign of its being much damaged. 'It's still a blank?' he asked. 'Your memory, I mean, of all that?'

Alice nodded dumbly, a picture of woe. When she did speak, it was with a sudden spurt of resentment. 'Look here,' she said, 'it's your job to clean up all this, isn't it? It's your job to find out what really happened, and why it happened, isn't it? Well – why don't you? Why don't you get us all out of our misery? I can't bear it any longer, I tell you – not knowing at all what it was that happened to Loo.'

'Yes, it's my job. Remember, though, that I haven't been on it very long.' Appleby spoke quietly. 'Even so, I don't think there will be much more waiting. You remember my saying how I hoped the mystery wouldn't last very far into today? Well, it won't. I've one or two people to get a little more information from. And then I think we can have – explanations.'

'That's really true?' Alice looked at him round-eyed, so that it was almost as if she were frightened again. 'But who? Who have you to get things from still?'

'The housekeeper, Mrs Husbands. And Rood.'

'The lawyer?' She spoke sharply. 'I don't trust that man. I said so before, didn't I? He's not straight.'

'Perhaps he's not. Unfortunately not many people in this affair have been quite as straight as they might have been. Look at these three precious worthies who were here a few minutes ago.'

'The Reverend's all right.'

'Perhaps so. But we needn't start checking up on the cast now, Alice. It's round about one o'clock in the morning, and you ought to be in bed. How do you feel? Shall I get hold of Mrs Husbands, or of Ruth?'

'I'm quite fit to look after myself, thank you.'

'Then I'll see you to your room. Come along.'

Alice stood up and shook her head. In country houses, she had doubtless read, it is not customary for ladies to be escorted to their bedrooms by gentlemen guests. 'You stay where you are,' she said firmly. 'But if I see you at breakfast, I'll be glad.'

Appleby smiled. 'I'll look out for you,' he said. 'And we'll try to sit together.'

Alice's footsteps quickly died away. Appleby lingered in Lewis Packford's library. He walked up and down, as the dead man must often have done when probing one or another of his literary problems. Perhaps Prodger was right in declaring the quiet of the night to be conducive to concentration. It was quiet enough now. There wasn't a sound throughout the house – and from beyond it there only came, very faintly, the occasional hooting of an owl. At 'The Crossed Hands' Rushout and the egregious Moody were presumably asleep. Or were they? Moody, at least, might be wakeful;

it was even rather surprising that, with his consuming mania for unique possessions, he was letting a night pass without laying actual siege to Urchins. But Moody, after all, was only on the fringe of the case. All the vital actors were under this roof, here and now.

Or was that right? Wasn't there something to be said, perhaps, for moving Moody, if not Rushout, a little nearer to the centre of the puzzle? As Appleby asked himself this question – still pacing softly up and down the silent library – he became aware of other questions obscurely redisposing themselves in his mind. And then he became aware that one, that another, that a third was evolving its own answer in the process. He already knew a lot; now he was learning that in fact, he knew significantly more.

For some minutes he was lost in profound abstraction. So deep was this, indeed, that when he was abruptly haled out of it by an unexpected sound in the night, it was a full second before he realized that that sound had been a revolver shot.

4

The shot hadn't been fired in the library or anywhere immediately adjoining it. And this was all that Appleby could say. He went to the door, threw it open, and listened. There wasn't a sound. But he couldn't conceivably be the only person still awake in Urchins; it seemed indeed improbable that any of the people who had so lately been in this room with him could be already asleep. They were hesitating, in fact, to be the first person to emerge and start the shouting. They were telling themselves that what they had heard was perhaps the fall of a picture or a looking-glass from the wall, or the backfire of a motor-bicycle in some nearby lane.

But now the silence was broken. It was broken, very faintly, by distant screams. And then he heard Edward Packford's voice, calm and authoritative, in some distant part of the house. 'Mrs Husbands – can you hear me? Tell those women to stop that noise and get back to bed.'

Well, that told one something at once. It was the housekeeper's domestic staff that had judged it incumbent upon itself to kick up a shindy. And as this part of the establishment was almost certainly accommodated in the attics, and as it must indeed have been abruptly roused from slumber thus to indulge in instant hysterics, the inference was that the shot had been fired at least as high as the main bedroom floor.

Appleby ran down the long corridor upon which the library gave, and then up the main staircase. A light went on as he reached the first landing, and he was just in time to see Edward Packford, in pyjamas and dressing-gown, emerge some distance away through a green baize door. Edward recognized him and strode forward. 'It was unmistakably a pistol-shot,' he said crisply. 'We'd better run it to earth before the real rumpus starts. It's my impression it was down here – past your own room in the east wing.' He turned to flick on more lights. 'Ah – there they go!'

It was certainly true that there they went. All over the house doors were now opening and voices calling. It must have been just like this, Appleby thought grimly, on the night Lewis Packford died. But on that occasion there hadn't been a policeman about the house. 'Would you please remember,' he asked Edward, 'not to touch any door-knobs with your bare hand? Use your handkerchief.'

Edward nodded, brought out a handkerchief, and threw open a door. He felt for the switch and turned on a light. 'A blank,' he said. 'Stupid of me. This one hardly ever is used. Try the one opposite.'

Appleby had already done so – and as the door swung back he became aware of a reek of gunpowder that told its own tale. 'The mischief's here,' he said. 'Would you mind stopping all those people from coming down this corridor?'

Edward turned back without a word; he seemed to acknowledge that it was Appleby's job to give orders. For a second Appleby stared into the enigmatical darkness ahead of him. He reached out for the light-switch – knowing that what was about to spring into visibility wouldn't be wholly unfamiliar to him. He had been here already that night.

Rood lay in a crumpled heap in the middle of the floor. Appleby crossed over to him and stooped down. In a second he knew that the solicitor was dead. The bullet had gone in at his right temple and out again at the base of the skull. The revolver lay by his limp right hand. It was a small and ineffective-looking affair. But it had killed Rood, all right. It had even made a distressing amount of mess.

Appleby went back to the door and glanced down the corridor. Nearly everybody seemed to be assembled at the end of it in a dishevelled and anxious group. Appleby walked towards them, his glance moving rapidly from one to another. 'I am very sorry to have to tell you,' he said quietly, 'that Mr Rood is dead. What we all heard appears to have been the revolver shot that killed him.'

There was a stunned silence. The first to speak was Canon Rixon. 'Do you mean,' he asked, 'that this unhappy man has taken his own life?'

Appleby shook his head. 'I am not the coroner and his jury, Dr Rixon. Rood has died – and rather as Lewis Packford died a few nights ago. I will say no more than that. And now, please, we must have the local police called at once. And, of course, a doctor. Mr Packford, will you see to that?'

Edward nodded. 'I'll get them on the telephone at once.'

'Thank you. Where is Mrs Husbands?'

'Mrs Husbands?' Edward seemed surprised. 'Isn't she here? But now I remember. I called out to her to go and quiet the servants. If you want her, I'll find her presently.'

'Perhaps Mrs Packford will be good enough to do so.' Appleby turned to Ruth. 'While Mr Packford is telephoning, will you find Mrs Husbands and bring her straight here?'

'Certainly.' Ruth hesitated. 'But you mean actually to – ?'

'Yes,' Appleby said, 'I do. She must be more or less used to violent death by now.'

Appleby went back to the dead man's room and took another look at the body. It was in pyjamas, and somehow it looked mean and meagre. The bedclothes were turned back – and in a fashion, it seemed to Appleby, that told a story. They hadn't simply been given the token turning-back that is part of a housemaid's ritual. They weren't, on the other hand, in any marked disorder. Rood was a man of neat and precise habits, who loved nothing more dearly than a well-rolled umbrella. He would get into bed without much disturbance. And if he had occasion to get out again, it would be just to this necessary extent that he would shove things away. If Rood had shot himself, he had got neatly and calmly out of bed to do so. If he had been shot by somebody else, it had been after getting out of bed in the same good order.

Appleby moved carefully around the room. The dead solicitor didn't appear to have done much unpacking. What was chiefly in evidence was a small pile of legal documents on a desk before a curtained window. Appleby looked at them closely. They were typewritten, but freely annotated in pencil. They seemed entirely concerned with Packford family affairs.

And then Appleby's glance travelled to the other end of the desk. A pencil lay on it; and beside the pencil was an irregular sheet of paper, such as might have been torn roughly out of a notebook. And on the paper was a pencilled scrawl. It read:

Farewell, a long farewell!

There was a knock at the door. Appleby turned away from the desk – he had spent a couple of further minutes there – and opened it to admit Mrs Husbands. The housekeeper too had presumably been in bed, but now she was dressed again, although hastily. She had daubed her face with powder – seemingly regardless of the fact that what it notably lacked was colour. Mrs Husbands, indeed, looked like a ghost; it was as if she had been abruptly translated from the Edwardian to a Stygian world. She was the second person, Appleby reflected, whom he had seen strangely transformed at Urchins that night.

'Please come in.' Appleby spoke gravely and with courtesy. 'I believe you can be of great assistance to me.'

He stood aside. Mrs Husbands hesitated. Her glance was going – half fearfully, half curiously – past him to the grim huddle of mortality on the floor. 'Must it be – here?' she asked.

'I am sorry to distress you. But I think it will be best.' Appleby closed the door behind the housekeeper. 'Let me be quite frank, Mrs Husbands. I am anxious that you should answer one or two questions at once – and before there has been any possibility of confusion.'

'Confusion, Sir John?'

'I think it possible that, were you now to engage in private consultation with another member of this household, a certain undesirable confusion might result.'

He could hear Mrs Husbands catch her breath. 'I do understand you,' she said. 'And I don't consider it proper to say anything without consulting Mr Packford, who is now my employer.'

'I certainly can't oblige you to talk.' Appleby had walked across the room, so that the dead body now lay sprawled between Mrs Husbands and himself. 'I am myself here as Mr Packford's guest. But I am also here officially, and at the invitation of the Chief Constable of this county. I cannot possibly venture to put any improper pressure upon you, even if I were anxious to do so. You may, if you wish, defer all discussion of what has happened in this house tonight, and all further discussion of what happened in it a few nights ago, until you have taken legal advice.'

'Then I shall certainly do so.'

'But I should like you to consider. I should like you to consider that, when one is faced with *this*' – and Appleby made an almost imperceptible gesture towards Rood's body – 'only the truth, and the immediate truth, is remotely adequate.'

'I don't know the truth. Anything I say may only lead fatally away from it.'

'That is very unlikely, Mrs Husbands. And you must consider that, where there have been two violent deaths, as in this house, the position becomes unpredictable and dangerous until the full truth is known. Concealment means danger – perhaps for yourself, perhaps for others.'

'Are you trying to frighten me, Sir John?'

'Conceivably I'm giving you a rational warning. And I can assure you that it is only a small number of questions which I should like you to answer. Will you come and look at something on this desk?' Appleby waited until she had crossed the room. 'It's rather like your experience of the other night, is it not?'

Mrs Husbands looked at the torn sheet of paper with its pencilled scrawl. 'You mean this?'

'Yes, I do. Have you seen it before?'

'But of course. It's the same message. Mr Rood has written the same words that Mr Packford did.'

'So it would appear. And I can't help feeling it was a little uninventive.'

Mrs Husbands frowned. 'Uninventive? I don't understand you.'

'He might have borrowed the first line of the same speech and written *So farewell to the little good you bear me.* Or, later on, I seem to recall a bit about swimming beyond one's depth. Would that, I wonder, have been appropriate?' Appleby paused, and then lightly touched the fragment of paper. 'But I think,' he said, 'that you may be said to have seen this before – in another sense?'

Mrs Husbands was silent.

'In fact, you have seen this actual piece of paper – either as it is now, or in its place in a notebook?'

'Yes, I have.' Suddenly in Mrs Husband's voice there was weariness and despair. 'Now, what more do you want of me?'

But Appleby shook his head. 'Nothing at all,' he said. 'My investigation is concluded.'

4

EPILOGUE IN THE WORKING LIBRARY
OF A SCHOLAR

Oh, most lame and impotent conclusion!

Othello

1

'Come in.'

Appleby spoke the words not by way of summons but as the beginning of an explanation. It was after breakfast, and everybody was in the library. Even Rushout and Moody were present – their arrival at Urchins having been hastened by a telephone call.

'*Come in.* Almost as soon as I heard the words, of course, I ought to have begun wondering what Lewis Packford was up to. For consider. His summer-house presented simply a blank wall on the side by which I approached it. So he couldn't possibly have spotted me – and indeed when I walked in he was clearly completely surprised. He assured me moreover that he was quite out of contact with either English men or English women. No doubt one might argue that, hearing a knock on a door, a man will instinctively call out in his own language. But that simply wouldn't be true in the particular circumstances of the case. Packford had fluent Italian, and he had been settled there at Garda for a good part of the summer. So you may put it this way. What would the reasonable inference have been if Packford had called out *Herein*?'

There was a moment's silence in the library, and then Edward Packford spoke a shade impatiently. 'One could be pretty sure that he was expecting a German, of course.'

'Precisely. His calling out in English was, admittedly, not so completely definitive as that. But at least it suggests a strong probability that your brother was expecting a visit from an Englishman.'

'Or from an American.' Limbrick, who had taken up a position from which he could glower offensively at Moody, made this suggestion with animus.

'Quite so. And Packford was certainly expecting somebody. Once or twice he looked at his watch in a way that wasn't wholly civil; and when I left him he was hurrying back to that summer-house like a man with an appointment. Thinking it over afterwards, I came to the conclusion that he had agreed to meet somebody quietly there either before one evening hour or after another one. That happened to make it possible for him to give me dinner at tolerable leisure – and to produce quite a lot of talk which later events have shown to be highly significant in itself. But even while talking he was distrait at times. So I didn't find it difficult to accept Rood's later suggestion that I had chanced to pay my call on Packford on the very evening that something extremely important was happening.' Appleby paused. 'In fact Rood's suggestion fitted in with my own sense of the whole incident. What was later to puzzle me a good deal was why Rood made it.'

'Puzzling conduct,' Ruth Packford said, 'appears to have been Mr Rood's forte. That, and howling bad taste. Whether he was a rascal or not, I don't know – and I don't greatly care. But to make his death a kind of grotesque echo of Lewis' was disgusting.'

Alice nodded approvingly. 'I quite agree with that, I must say. Leaving the same message – about the long farewell, I mean – was in bad taste. It wasn't a thing a gentleman would do.'

'I suppose,' Edward Packford asked, 'that the handwriting will prove to be authentically Rood's?'

'I'm quite sure it will.' Appleby spoke with authority. 'He had been annotating some legal documents, so I've been able to make a comparison. Rood wrote the scrawl we found last night.'

'Echoing what my brother wrote?'

Appleby shook his head. 'Your brother never wrote anything of the sort. Both these messages were written by Rood.'

There was a baffled silence. And it was Ruth's mind which first got to work effectively on Appleby's announcement. 'In other words,' she said, 'Lewis was never by way of saying farewell to anybody or anything?'

'Precisely. I had to consider, of course, the possibility that he had been killed immediately after writing something merely designed to announce that he was solving his difficult matrimonial situation – if that's the right word for it – by packing up and clearing out. The suitcase which turned up in his car seemed for a time to support that interpretation. But the suitcase was Alice's work. I am inclined to think that, during the period of total loss of memory which she has described, she visited Packford in this room and suggested flight. Then, still in the same dissociated state, she packed a suitcase for him and hid it in his car, together with the little travelling-case of her own. I've already explained this hypothesis to Alice, and she doesn't disagree with it. All this, of course, wasn't a confusion upon which Rood could have been reckoning at all. But it was otherwise with the simple arrival of the two ladies at Urchins and the crisis which that produced. Rood certainly engineered that. It was an essential part of his plan. Or rather it was an essential part of one of his plans. For he had a great belief in keeping things flexible. It was a trait which emerged in my first conversation with him. You might call it his Napoleon complex. That in turn was a reflex of his vanity. And these elements are at the heart of the case.'

'Are we to understand, then,' Canon Rixon asked, 'that this unfortunate solicitor was throughout prosecuting some criminal design? This is shocking indeed.'

'You are to understand, for a start, that he planned an elaborate, foolish and conceited hoax.'

'A hoax?' Edward Packford's voice was sharp, and he had swung round on Appleby. 'Just what do you mean by that?'

'You will understand what I mean presently. And it is better, I think, to speak of a hoax than of a fraud – at least in the first instance. But let me go back to Garda. I left your brother, so to speak, expecting an English visitor – and concealing the fact of that expectation from a casual caller in the person of myself. Well, yesterday I discovered – and in rather an odd way – that that English visitor had almost certainly been Rood himself. You will agree, I think, that your brother had rather a simple sense of humour, and was moreover fond of repeating his little jokes?'

Edward nodded. 'Perfectly true.'

'When I called on him, he happened to remark upon the decoration of his summer-house. There were wall paintings of a somewhat insipid erotic cast. He referred to them as amorous shrimps, and added that there was no vice in them. When I happened, in this connection, to repeat the phrase "amorous shrimps" to Rood, Rood at once, in speaking of your brother, used the phrase "no vice in him" to me. The associative link was unmistakable. Rood too had heard that joke from your brother in the summer-house. But Rood had implicitly denied ever having visited your brother at Garda. He had simply corresponded with him, and arranged for the transfer of £1,000 – the sum required, according to Rood's story, to buy some valuable book or document from an impoverished nobleman of Verona. It became clear to me that this impoverished nobleman was moonshine. Rood had invented him; and had persuaded your brother that he, Rood, was acting as an intermediary in delicate negotiations.'

There was silence again – oddly broken by a burst of rather harsh laughter from Rushout. 'Is this leading up to the proposition that the supposed annotations by Shakespeare in that *Ecatommiti* are a fake – a forgery?'

'Certainly it is. Rood was a bit of a scholar and a bit of a palaeographer. And Lewis Packford – Mr Packford here has told me – used to rather laugh at Rood's pretensions, and indeed to make fun of him generally. With a man of Rood's temperament, that was a dangerous thing to do. And Rood furthermore possessed a dangerous accomplishment: he had made himself into a brilliant forger. Not, of course, of his clients' signatures on cheques, or anything of that sort; but simply in the field of literary and antiquarian investigation. The history of scholarship is oddly full of that sort of thing; and there are all degrees of the impulse. The learned joke about Bogdown, if I may venture to say so, is a sort of first-cousin to it.'

Canon Rixon raised a mildly protesting hand at this. 'My dear Sir John, I consider that remark to be contentious. But proceed.'

'Rood, then, determined on a shattering hoax at Packford's expense. On the one hand, he counted on his own quite exceptional skill; and on the other, on what may be called a sanguine streak in his proposed victim. He told me that he regarded Packford as credulous. Even so, his proposed deception was a great gamble. But then he admired gambles. He told me that too. And he particularly admired the gambler who will double his stake at a crisis. The relevance of that will appear later.'

Appleby paused to look round his auditory. With the exception of Alice, who had clearly given up trying to grasp what it was all about, they were as attentive as any actor or lecturer could wish. Moody, who had perhaps been hurried over his breakfast, was covertly swallowing one of Dr Cahoon's pills. But nobody else moved.

'The hoax might have worked. As we all now know, Packford went so far as to write a letter to Professor Rushout, stating his conviction that he had found an incomparably important body of marginalia by Shakespeare. And he dropped various hints about it to other people now in this library. The time had come for Rood to disclose the truth, and set the whole learned world laughing at Lewis Packford's gullibility. Unfortunately Rood had, at quite an early stage, allowed himself one of those swift changes of plan he was so proud of. He had admitted a simple profit motive into his enterprise, and collected from his victim a large sum of money – ostensibly to hand over to the impoverished Veronese nobleman. This, when you come to think of it, was really a hopeless and pitiable muddle at the start. For it would only be for so long as the authenticity of the marginalia went virtually unquestioned that there would be no danger of investigations which would ultimately expose the whole Veronese story as a fraud. Rood could, of course, have handed back the £1,000 at the moment of exploding his hoax. But clearly he didn't want to. So he thought again, and changed his strategy once more.'

Again Appleby paused, and again for a moment nobody moved. But then Limbrick struck a match and lit a cigarette. 'I can't see,' he said easily, 'that you aren't possibly making all this up. About the spuriousness, I mean, of the marginalia in the *Ecatommiti*. Let us admit that Rood was in Italy. But he may genuinely have been acting as a go-between, in relation to a genuine nobleman owning a genuine Shakespearian treasure. So far, you have been importing the notion of forgery simply on the strength of your own reading of Rood's character.'

Appleby nodded. 'There's some truth in that. If I were a barrister, presenting this material in court, I should have to begin by ordering my entire material much more carefully. As it is, I'm assuming things that can only appear incontestable a little later on, when the rest of the evidence is fitted into place. You'll find, that's to say, that matters to which I shall presently come are not reconcilable with the assumption that the marginalia are genuine.'

At this Rushout took it upon himself to nod judiciously. 'So far,' he said, 'your case at least possesses what I'd call internal coherence. And I'm prepared myself to believe the damned stuff is bogus. If only' – he sighed – 'because it's too good to be true.'

'Very well. And I've now come to a point at which Rood, as I conceive the matter, began to evolve a really formidable battery of alternative plans. He had found out about the embarrassing matrimonial dilemma which his client and victim had fallen into. Mr Packford here had advised his brother to take legal advice, and so Lewis Packford had told Rood the story. Rood's instinct would be to exploit it in some way. And in one set of eventualities, he saw, a descent by the ladies upon Urchins might afford a useful element of confusion. So he communicated with them anonymously, and saw to it that they presented themselves here virtually simultaneously. He himself came down to Urchins at the same time.'

Edward Packford raised his head at this. 'Did he? We certainly knew nothing about it.'

'I understand that it was your brother's invariable habit to spend an hour or two in this library before going to bed. Rood had no need to announce himself. On a summer evening, he could simply walk in by the French window. And that is what he did.'

'Intending murder?'

'Almost certainly not. Indeed, I'm not positively certain that he intended to confront your brother at all. It seems to me conceivable that he simply intended to slip into the house and conceal himself. The plan at this time in the forefront of his mind was probably theft. And that is where Mr Moody comes in.'

'Huh?' This was the first sound that Moody had uttered.

'The position, remember, was this. Lewis Packford had possessed himself of these supposed marginalia by Shakespeare. He had informed Professor Rushout about them, and he had dropped hints to other people. Packford, of course, was a great name in this particular field of learning, and his opinion would carry much weight. When, however, the marginalia were eventually given to the world, they would almost certainly be questioned, debated and eventually exposed. That was no longer what Rood desired, or looked forward to as other than thoroughly inconvenient. But if he could possess himself of the Cintio again – steal it, in fact – he could dispose of it to that sort of collector who doesn't object to clandestine acquisitions, and who indeed has rather a fancy for them. Mr Moody certainly falls into that category. He has a fancy for possessing remarkable things that nobody knows about. He told me so himself. Isn't that right, Mr Moody?'

Moody considered this question sombrely for a moment. 'Huh,' he said.

'Quite so. And let us notice that Mr Moody would be paying a substantial sum for the marginalia on the strength of the conviction which Lewis Packford had arrived at about it, while at the same time being unable, in the nature of the case, to call in further expert opinion by way of corroboration. Rood, then, had a lot to gain by simply walking off with the Cintio if he could lay his hands on it.'

Professor Prodger, who had for some time given the appearance of slumbering within the recesses of his venerable beard, was prompted to speech by this. 'But that mightn't be easy – eh? That mightn't be easy, at all. Even if he had the advantage of knowing the precise book he was looking for. Am I right, Rixon? Limbrick, would you agree with me?'

Appleby nodded. 'That is obviously true. And there is no doubt that Rood did in fact have an interview with Lewis Packford here in the library. And there is equally little doubt that Packford produced the Cintio. Rood's simplest way of finding out where it was kept would be to contrive this. Unfortunately he found out something else as well. Perhaps you can guess what that was.'

'That Lewis knew the truth, after all?' It was Ruth Packford who asked this. She had been following Appleby with absolute concentration.

'Certainly that he knew a great deal of the truth. Your husband, that is to say, had detected the fact of forgery. He had done so, it may be, only within the preceding few hours; and without doubt he had, so far, communicated his discovery to no one. There seems a high probability that Rood had underestimated his victim's intelligence right from the start. Packford had indeed been bowled over by the magnitude of the supposed find, so that for a time his critical faculties were in abeyance. But from the first I believe that doubts and suspicions were gnawing at his mind – even without his being at all consciously aware of it. The drift of our conversation at Garda seems to me highly significant now. He talked about the technique of literary forgery – old paper, a chemically correct ink and so forth – and also about its psychology: forgery sometimes starting as a joke, gratifying an impulse to laugh up one's sleeve, being particularly attractive to those who have reason to suppose themselves patronized or looked down upon. Very obscurely, in fact, his mind was groping after the basis of the whole deception which was being launched against him at that very moment. And now some more minute study of his find flashed on him the truth that it was spurious.'

'And you think,' Ruth asked, 'that he taxed Rood there and then?'

'No, I don't. I think his first supposition was that both he and Rood had been equally the victims of an imposture. But you see the crisis with which Rood suddenly found himself confronted. Once

Packford had communicated his revised opinion to Professor Rushout, or anybody of the sort, the Cintio would become virtually valueless. So there was no point in stealing it. And, whether he stole it or not, Lewis Packford would certainly conduct an investigation as a consequence of which he himself could scarcely escape exposure. Nor would he then be able to plead that he had been devising a harmless and even salutary hoax. For the cold fact would be that he had fabricated a false document, invented a false provenance for it, and sold it for a large sum of money. Things were turning very awkward for him. It was incumbent upon him, therefore, to bring one of his reserve plans into operation. Fortunately he had – or believed himself to have – a Napoleonic genius in that direction.'

'And so,' Edward Packford asked, 'we come to murder?'

'And so we come to murder – and to a little more forgery. It is obvious that, if your brother died there and then, with the fact of his final discovery of the spuriousness of the marginalia undisclosed, Rood could still do very well. He could walk off with the Cintio, just as he had already proposed. Later, Professor Rushout would certainly make public the fact that Packford had believed himself to be in possession of important Shakespeare marginalia; there would be a vain hunt for the missing volume; and Rood would have something pleasingly notorious to peddle to Mr Moody on the quiet.'

'Huh.'

'And already the way was paved for this alternative operation. Acute domestic embarrassment had been, so to speak, dumped on the doorstep of Urchins that very afternoon. If Lewis Packford was given the appearance of committing suicide there and then, there would be a ready-made motive. So Rood shot him, and scrawled that note. He had, of course, put in a lot of time perfecting his command of Packford's handwriting. I think it likely that he was ingenious enough to use a particularly slow-drying ink – in the hope that the first person brought to the spot by the shot would notice this apparently incontestable piece of additional evidence.'

167

There was a scrape of a match as Limbrick lit another cigarette. 'And this,' he said, 'is the point at which your whole case, Sir John, turns to sheer nonsense. You say that Rood committed murder and ingeniously disguised it as suicide. But everybody knows that he was later virtually the only person to declare that it *was* murder. Do you maintain that he was simply putting up a crazy double bluff?'

Appleby shook his head. 'Not quite that. The Napoleonic change of plan had a fatal attraction for Rood simply, one may say, for its own sake. It cropped up in his conversation in a way that clearly indicated an obsession. But there was, at the same time, a rational basis for this very hazardous second – or third – thought, when he embarked upon it. And this again concerns our American friend, Mr Moody, who has so kindly come along this morning.'

Limbrick blew out a cloud of cigarette-smoke. 'Huh,' he said impudently.

'Huh?' Moody eyed Limbrick aggressively. Then, perhaps warned by some interior spasm, he reached for his pills again. 'Huh,' he said.

'The point was this,' Appleby went on. 'The Cintio had appeared obscurely, and it had been changing hands obscurely. If it had left in its wake, so to speak, nothing more serious than a suicide, Mr Moody or some similar purchaser might have risked coming out into the open with it, after all. Once it was heard about, it would almost certainly be examined by experts, and the danger of its being proved a fake would be very real – so that once more Rood might be booked for trouble. Murder is a different matter. Once any strong suspicion that Packford had been murdered got abroad – once it was known that the police were seriously pursuing the possibility, and so forth – then it would become a very dubious and dangerous possession indeed, and its new owner would almost certainly keep quiet about it. Hence Rood's new attitude. He lay in wait for me – I can now see – after Packford's funeral, and began airing a theory of murder and robbery. Indeed he had already begun on that line with my colleague Cavill – expressing his conviction, for instance, that the message on the postcard was a forgery. Later he was to assure me that it was a *brilliant* forgery – which is a pretty enough instance of the operation of his very large conceit. And of course it was Rood who got yesterday's evening papers to turn Packford's death into a sensation and reveal that I had come down to investigate. Perhaps he knew, by the time he did this, that Mr Moody had actually arrived in England. And here, incidentally, we come to a yet more compelling reason for Rood's turning Packford's death into murder. There's just nothing that Mr Moody likes better than that sort of thing. He has a remarkable collection of more or less blood-streaked relics. Isn't that so, Mr Moody?'

'Huh?' Moody considered for a moment, and then appeared to resolve on speech. 'Sure,' he said.

'And the collection is growing all the time?'

'Sure. I can get those things when I want them. I can get most anything when I want it.'

'Exactly. That, if I may say so, is a most succinct statement of your position. And when you read in the English papers last night a lot of stuff about Lewis Packford's having been murdered, you wanted his Cintio even more than you'd wanted it before?'

'Sure. That's only sense, isn't it?'

'Of course it is.' Appleby nodded with conviction. 'In addition to all those scribblings by Shakespeare, the book would have this further associational interest. I believe that's the term. And now we're almost finished with Rood. But not quite.'

Canon Rixon shook his head. 'And, meantime, the wretched man is finished with us. I am bound to say I think it's to his credit. The Archbishop would no doubt disagree with me. And of course theological considerations must not be ignored. Still, Rood has, so to speak, taken himself off before a great deal of horrible degradation in courts of law. I admire his courage.'

Appleby was silent for a moment. 'I at least admire his cleverness – and the less reluctantly, perhaps because it was, in a last analysis, of such a crack-brained sort. One can't, in my line of territory, afford to admire anything at all in a really tiptop and thoroughly capable criminal. But those on the lunatic fringe one can extend a little charity to, even when their cleverness has drawn them into horrible crime. But that's by the way. I now come to the second stage of my investigation.'

'You certainly seem disposed to give us good measure.' Edward Packford had risen to his feet and strolled to the window. Now he was surveying the whole company with a speculative eye. 'There's more to come? Something more lies behind Rood's taking the course he did?'

'What lies behind it,' Limbrick said, 'is presumably the good Sir John's chasing him up – chasing him up with what I myself would still describe as a wonderfully convincing fantasy. Perhaps Rood judged it so convincing that he didn't see much hope in the mere fact of its being a high-class policeman's fairy-tale. And that would be too bad.'

Alice, who had continued mute during the further intricacies of Appleby's exposition, was suddenly prompted to make a purely human remark. 'All this would be a little *less* bad,' she said to Limbrick, 'if you kept your bloody mouth shut.'

'I thoroughly agree,' Prodger sat up so suddenly that a couple of startled moths flew out of his beard. 'Limbrick, having been humilatingly exposed in reprehensible courses not many hours ago, ought in mere decency to be silent.' He turned to Alice. 'Nor, my dear young woman, need you blush at so legitimate a use of the resources of the vulgar tongue. Sir John, proceed.'

'Thank you. Well, the final stage of the affair turns on the fact that Rood liked, as he expressed it to me, to be ready for all eventualities. Even, apparently, for tolerably unlikely ones. He may have got wind of the fact that Mr Moody – whose reputation and habits I discovered to be well known to him – was in this country. But when Rood returned to Urchins yesterday with Packford's will and so forth, he can surely have seen only a remote chance of Moody's actually being here or in the neighbourhood. Nevertheless Rood was prepared for that, as for other things. He brought two suitcases with him.'

'So he did.' Ruth Packford nodded. 'I noticed them when we collected him from the railway station.'

'Quite so. And you may have noticed something more. They were *twin* suitcases.' Appleby smiled grimly. 'And that is something which no Napoleon should provide himself with.'

'Do you mean,' Rushout asked curiously, 'because they can get muddled up?'

'Just that. But now I must say something about Mrs Husbands. I see she isn't here in the library, so I can begin with a well-deserved compliment. Amid all these alarms, the household over which she presides continues to run very smoothly.'

Rixon nodded emphatically. 'I quite agree. If the cook, for example, has been discomposed at any time the circumstance has never been allowed to impinge upon our host's table. And that is truly remarkable, we shall all agree.'

Appleby nodded. 'It is more immediately relevant to my own argument, however, that the house-maiding seems to remain equally efficient. My own suitcase was unpacked for me in the most orthodox way. But Rood's was not.'

Edward Packford came back from the window and sat down again. 'I'm afraid,' he said mildly, 'that's it's too late to apologize to him. But is the circumstance highly relevant?'

'As it happens, it is. Yesterday evening, and by mere chance, I became aware of Mrs Husbands coming out of what later revealed itself as Rood's bedroom. She came out as if anxious not to be seen doing so. That was rather odd. But much odder was the fact that she appeared to be in a state of shock, and even perhaps terror. I resolved to investigate the matter as soon as I had an opportunity. It was thus that I later came upon Rood preparing to go to bed. I had a conversation with him, which I found interesting in several particulars. But much more interesting was something I simply *saw* as soon as I opened the door. Rood was standing by one of his suitcases, and fishing out a pair of pyjamas. Why hadn't this job been done for him, as it had been done for me? There was an obvious answer. He had forgotten to unlock the suitcase containing his clothes. But this could scarcely in itself have had a shattering effect upon Mrs Husbands, who had presumably been going round the house to see that everything of that sort had been attended to. There must be some other explanation. And that other explanation was clear. Rood had failed to unlock the *right* suitcase simply because he had in fact unlocked the *wrong* one. Its contents had been unpromising, and the housemaid had retired baffled. But Mrs Husbands had investigated. And she had come upon something that completely shattered her. To put the point crudely, she did a little covert rummaging among Rood's possessions – and her action was the proximate cause of Rood's death.'

Edward Packford had stood up again. 'It seems to me,' he said seriously, 'that this is a very grave statement. If the matter is to be taken further now, I think Mrs Husbands should be present. Shall I fetch her?'

For a fraction of a second Appleby hesitated. Then he nodded. 'Yes, do,' he said.

Edward moved to the door. 'I presume,' he asked, 'that you have already had some talk with her about this queer development?'

'I had some talk with her very shortly after Rood's death.'

'And she admitted finding something shattering – I think that was your word – in the suitcase which Rood had so rashly unlocked?'

'She did.'

Edward nodded. 'She ought not to have rummaged. I'm surprised at her. Still, if it helps to clear things up – as you seem to think it does – nobody's going to blame the lady. I'll find her right away.'

Edward left the library, and there was a long silence. It was broken – rather nervously – by Rushout. 'You say that Moody's being here was an eventuality for which this unfortunate and bloody-minded solicitor had arrived prepared. And you have spun us this yarn about a right and a wrong suitcase. I take it he had brought the Cintio back with him? It was what Mrs Husbands stumbled on?'

'He had certainly brought the Cintio back with him.' Appleby spoke out of what appeared to be a profound and sombre abstraction.

'Then I must say he had a nerve. He was proposing, if the opportunity offered, actually to do a deal with Moody here on the spot?'

'Just that. When I told him that Mr Moody would be around in the morning, Rood said very happily that in that case he'd make bold to stop at Urchins a little longer than he had intended to. He and Moody, he said, would certainly have a chat.' Appleby smiled faintly. 'He was wrong about that.'

'I can only repeat: he had a nerve.'

There was a long, awkward silence. Then Appleby appeared to rouse himself. 'A nerve? Well, yes. He drew my attention to the fact that the faking of a suicide for Lewis Packford had been a palpably false step, likely to direct investigation into a very narrow field: that of persons who could conceivably bring off the forgery on that postcard. Or words to that effect. He was a bold criminal, without a doubt.'

'Edward must be having difficulty in finding Mrs Husbands.' Ruth spoke casually – but with one hand she was nervously tapping the arm of her chair.

'Yes,' Appleby said.

Limbrick made to light another cigarette, and then appeared to think better of it. Alice's broadside had shaken him. Alice herself appeared to be uneasy – which was no doubt the reason why Canon Rixon had taken once more to a fatherly patting of her hand. Prodger was perhaps asleep. Moody was glancing about the library – warily, but at the same time with the assurance of a man who gets most anything he wants. And then the door opened and Mrs Husbands came in.

She was alone. She shut the door behind her, and looked round the room. She was carrying a book in an ancient leather binding. She walked up to Ruth and put the book down on a table beside her. 'Mr Packford,' she said, in a strained voice, 'asked me to give you this. He asked me to say that of course it is yours – and that he is sorry it isn't worth much.'

Ruth glanced at the book, and then swiftly from Mrs Husbands to Appleby. 'But where is he?' she asked. 'Where is Edward?'

Nobody had a reply. And then, in the instant's silence, in some distant part of the house, there rang out a single pistol-shot.

Alice was the first to spring to her feet. 'What is it?' she cried. 'What was that?'

Appleby too rose. 'I am afraid,' he said quietly, 'that it is another long farewell. The last.'

It was a couple of hours later, and Appleby and Ruth Packford were alone in the garden.

'You let him go and do it,' she said. 'I think I admire that – taking the responsibility, I mean, of letting him go. But I suppose that, in a policeman, it wasn't quite regular. You ought to have arrested him. And endless horrors ought to have followed. Do they hang people nowadays? I forget.'

Appleby made no reply. They walked on. The morning was faintly autumnal, and already sycamore and chestnut leaves were falling on the fringes of the lawn. 'I wonder,' Appleby said, 'what happens to this place now? Is it all tied up, so that some distant Packford has to be found to take it over? Or does it come to you?'

'Rood would know.' Ruth made a long pause. 'Why did he kill Lewis? It was madness. It was an absurdity.'

'Yes, it was. And the only real answer is that he thought it clever. Of course he was going to make money out of Moody, and all that. But it was his own cleverness he was in love with.'

'And Edward?'

'He was devoted to Lewis. I remember, early on, a sudden fire in him when he said he wished he had been here when Lewis was killed. He meant that the mere intensity of his feeling would have directed him to be killed. And he said something even more revealing about his having a flair for summary justice. Or something of the sort. But one must realize – if one is to get the simple moral issues of this ghastly business straight – that Edward Packford committed precisely as grave a crime as Rood. He fancied himself as an embodiment of justice. Or, if you prefer it, he fancied himself as a public executioner. He judged Rood, and he put Rood to death. Well, he had no business to. He was a murderer. He would have been a murderer, even if his motive hadn't been, in actual fact, vitiated and corrupt.'

'You mean that Edward had a profit motive, as well as a notion of executing justice?'

'Certainly he had. He was going to kill two birds with one stone – and feather his own nest on the proceeds.' Appleby's voice had an unwonted hardness. 'He was lucky to be let blow his own brains out. And there's an end to it.'

'Very well. There's an end of it. But there are still things I don't understand.'

'Not many, I imagine. You see, Rood had with him in that second suitcase what you might call his whole bag of tricks. Mrs Husbands may have seen the Cintio – but I doubt whether it would have conveyed much to her. What she certainly did see – as she admitted to me finally last night – was a notebook of Rood's. It contained, jotted down in his hand, a number of appropriate Shakespeare quotations which might have been useful as last messages. Mrs Husbands opened the thing straight on *Farewell, a long farewell.* No wonder that she was staggered. She went straight to Edward and told him of her discovery. He went at once to Rood's bedroom and found not only the notebook but the Cintio. This, I believe, was while I was having some talk with Alice. When I subsequently saw Edward, he was a changed man. He had realized almost the whole truth about his brother's death. And presently he was to glimpse a tremendous tempation.'

'The Cintio?'

'Yes. Remember that Urchins isn't at all flourishing, and that he was left with the task of keeping it up without his brother's purely personal fortune, which comes to you. It was an inconvenient sort of inheritance. The precise nature of the book – Cintio's *Ecatommiti* with its marginalia – was real news to him; and he at once understood its value. He also knew about Moody, who would give an enormous sum for such a thing even if it had to remain an absolutely secret part of his collection. Moreover he felt – Edward felt – that justice required that he, Edward, should have it. Edward, as we have seen, was very strong on justice. It's what's killed him.'

Ruth shivered. 'Yes,' she said, 'I see that. But you know, he'd only have had to ask me for the damned book. Wouldn't he know that?'

'Apparently not. His case was – these were his own words to me – that you were entitled to anything you had a reasonable expectation of. And that didn't include this enormously valuable discovery of his brother's. So he avenged his brother and stole from him – or from you – in one and the same act. He killed Rood, left on his table the ripped-out page from the notebook, and made off with the *Ecatommiti*. He still didn't know of course, that it was a forgery. And even when that disconcerting truth broke on him this morning, he still thought he was all right. It was only when he learnt I had got Mrs Husbands' story that he realized it was all up with him.'

Ruth shook her head. She looked dazed and weary. They turned back towards the house. 'At least it's over,' she said. 'A ghastly story. Is there a moral to it?'

Appleby thought for a moment. 'There's no moral. There's only a caution.'

'And that is?'

'When you're in the middle of Italy, think twice when a voice calls "Come in".'

MICHAEL INNES

APPLEBY AT ALLINGTON

Sir John Appleby dines one evening at Allington Park, the Georgian home of his acquaintance, Owain Allington, who is new to the area. His curiosity is aroused when Allington mentions his nephew and heir to the estate, Martin Allington, whose name Appleby recognises. The evening comes to an end but, just as Appleby is leaving, they find a dead man – electrocuted in the *son et lumière* box that had been installed in the grounds.

APPLEBY ON ARARAT

Inspector Appleby is stranded on a very strange island, with a rather odd bunch of people – too many men, too few women (and one of them too attractive) cause a deal of trouble. But that is nothing compared to later developments, including the body afloat in the water and the attack by local inhabitants.

'Every sentence he writes has flavour, every incident flamboyance'
– *The Times Literary Supplement*

MICHAEL INNES

THE DAFFODIL AFFAIR

Inspector Appleby's aunt is most distressed when her horse, Daffodil – a somewhat half-witted animal with exceptional numerical skills – goes missing from her stable in Harrogate. Meanwhile, Hudspith is hot on the trail of Lucy Rideout, an enigmatic young girl who has been whisked away to an unknown isle by a mysterious gentleman. And when a house in Bloomsbury, supposedly haunted, also goes missing, the baffled policemen search for a connection. As Appleby and Hudspith trace Daffodil and Lucy, the fragments begin to come together and an extravagant project is uncovered, leading them to a South American jungle.

'Yet another surprising firework display of wit and erudition and ingenious invention' – *The Guardian*

DEATH AT THE PRESIDENT'S LODGING

Inspector Appleby is called to St Anthony's College, where the President has been murdered in his Lodging. Scandal abounds when it becomes clear that the only people with any motive to murder him are the only people who had the opportunity – because the President's Lodging opens off Orchard Ground, which is locked at night, and only the Fellows of the College have keys…

'It is quite the most accomplished first crime novel that I have read…all first-rate entertainment' – Cecil Day Lewis, *The Daily Telegraph*

MICHAEL INNES

HAMLET, REVENGE!

At Seamnum Court, seat of the Duke of Horton, The Lord Chancellor of England is murdered at the climax of a private presentation of *Hamlet*, in which he plays Polonius. Inspector Appleby pursues some of the most famous names in the country, unearthing dreadful suspicion.

'Michael Innes is in a class by himself among writers of detective fiction' – *The Times Literary Supplement*

A PRIVATE VIEW

Sir John and Lady Appleby attend a memorial exhibition of the oils, gouaches, collages and *trouvailles* of artist Gavin Limbert, who was recently found shot under very suspicious circumstances. As Assistant-Commissioner of Police, Sir John is already interested, but he becomes even more intrigued when Limbert's last masterpiece is stolen from the gallery under his very eyes.

'Exciting, amusingly written…very good enjoyment it is' – *The Spectator*

TITLES BY MICHAEL INNES AVAILABLE DIRECT
FROM HOUSE OF STRATUS

Quantity		£	$(US)	€
	THE AMPERSAND PAPERS	6.99	9.95	13.50
	APPLEBY AND HONEYBATH	6.99	9.95	13.50
	APPLEBY AND THE OSPREYS	6.99	9.95	13.50
	APPLEBY AT ALLINGTON	6.99	9.95	13.50
	THE APPLEBY FILE	6.99	9.95	13.50
	APPLEBY ON ARARAT	6.99	9.95	13.50
	APPLEBY PLAYS CHICKEN	6.99	9.95	13.50
	APPLEBY TALKING	6.99	9.95	13.50
	APPLEBY TALKS AGAIN	6.99	9.95	13.50
	APPLEBY'S ANSWER	6.99	9.95	13.50
	APPLEBY'S END	6.99	9.95	13.50
	APPLEBY'S OTHER STORY	6.99	9.95	13.50
	AN AWKWARD LIE	6.99	9.95	13.50
	THE BLOODY WOOD	6.99	9.95	13.50
	CARSON'S CONSPIRACY	6.99	9.95	13.50
	A CHANGE OF HEIR	6.99	9.95	13.50
	CHRISTMAS AT CANDLESHOE	6.99	9.95	13.50
	A CONNOISSEUR'S CASE	6.99	9.95	13.50
	THE DAFFODIL AFFAIR	6.99	9.95	13.50
	DEATH AT THE CHASE	6.99	9.95	13.50
	DEATH AT THE PRESIDENT'S LODGING	6.99	9.95	13.50
	A FAMILY AFFAIR	6.99	9.95	13.50
	FROM LONDON FAR	6.99	9.95	13.50
	THE GAY PHOENIX	6.99	9.95	13.50

ALL HOUSE OF STRATUS BOOKS ARE AVAILABLE FROM GOOD BOOKSHOPS
OR DIRECT FROM THE PUBLISHER:

Internet: www.houseofstratus.com including synopses and features.

Email: sales@houseofstratus.com
              info@houseofstratus.com
              (please quote author, title and credit card details.)

TITLES BY MICHAEL INNES AVAILABLE DIRECT
FROM HOUSE OF STRATUS

Quantity		£	$(US)	€
	GOING IT ALONE	6.99	9.95	13.50
	HAMLET, REVENGE!	6.99	9.95	13.50
	HARE SITTING UP	6.99	9.95	13.50
	HONEYBATH'S HAVEN	6.99	9.95	13.50
	THE JOURNEYING BOY	6.99	9.95	13.50
	LAMENT FOR A MAKER	6.99	9.95	13.50
	LORD MULLION'S SECRET	6.99	9.95	13.50
	THE MAN FROM THE SEA	6.99	9.95	13.50
	MONEY FROM HOLME	6.99	9.95	13.50
	THE MYSTERIOUS COMMISSION	6.99	9.95	13.50
	THE NEW SONIA WAYWARD	6.99	9.95	13.50
	A NIGHT OF ERRORS	6.99	9.95	13.50
	OLD HALL, NEW HALL	6.99	9.95	13.50
	THE OPEN HOUSE	6.99	9.95	13.50
	OPERATION PAX	6.99	9.95	13.50
	A PRIVATE VIEW	6.99	9.95	13.50
	THE SECRET VANGUARD	6.99	9.95	13.50
	SHEIKS AND ADDERS	6.99	9.95	13.50
	SILENCE OBSERVED	6.99	9.95	13.50
	STOP PRESS	6.99	9.95	13.50
	THERE CAME BOTH MIST AND SNOW	6.99	9.95	13.50
	THE WEIGHT OF THE EVIDENCE	6.99	9.95	13.50
	WHAT HAPPENED AT HAZELWOOD	6.99	9.95	13.50

ALL HOUSE OF STRATUS BOOKS ARE AVAILABLE FROM GOOD BOOKSHOPS
OR DIRECT FROM THE PUBLISHER:

Tel:	Order Line 0800 169 1780 (UK) International +44 (0) 1845 527700 (UK)
Fax:	+44 (0) 1845 527711 (UK) (please quote author, title and credit card details.)
Send to:	House of Stratus Sales Department Thirsk Industrial Park York Road, Thirsk North Yorkshire, YO7 3BX UK

PAYMENT

Please tick currency you wish to use:

☐ £ (Sterling)　　　☐ $ (US)　　　☐ € (Euros)

Allow for shipping costs charged per order plus an amount per book as set out in the tables below:

CURRENCY/DESTINATION

	£(Sterling)	$(US)	€ (Euros)
Cost per order			
UK	1.50	2.25	2.50
Europe	3.00	4.50	5.00
North America	3.00	3.50	5.00
Rest of World	3.00	4.50	5.00
Additional cost per book			
UK	0.50	0.75	0.85
Europe	1.00	1.50	1.70
North America	1.00	1.00	1.70
Rest of World	1.50	2.25	3.00

PLEASE SEND CHEQUE OR INTERNATIONAL MONEY ORDER payable to: HOUSE OF STRATUS LTD or card payment as indicated

STERLING EXAMPLE

Cost of book(s):..................... Example: 3 x books at £6.99 each: £20.97

Cost of order:...................... Example: £1.50 (Delivery to UK address)

Additional cost per book:.............. Example: 3 x £0.50: £1.50

Order total including shipping:........... Example: £23.97

VISA, MASTERCARD, SWITCH, AMEX:

☐☐☐☐☐☐☐☐☐☐☐☐☐☐☐☐☐☐☐☐

Issue number (Switch only):

☐☐☐

Start Date:　　　　　　　　**Expiry Date:**

☐☐/☐☐　　　　　　　　☐☐/☐☐

Signature: _____

NAME: _____

ADDRESS: _____

COUNTRY: _____

ZIP/POSTCODE: _____

Please allow 28 days for delivery. Despatch normally within 48 hours.

Prices subject to change without notice.
Please tick box if you do not wish to receive any additional information. ☐

House of Stratus publishes many other titles in this genre; please check our website (**www.houseofstratus.com**) for more details.